Been So Long 2

(Body and Soul)

Adrienne Thompson

Pink Cashmere Publishing Company

Cover art from dreamstime.com

Cover by Adrienne Thompson

Edited by Alyndria Mooney

Printed in the United States of America

First Printing 2013

Copyright © 2013 Adrienne Thompson

ISBN: 0988871327

ISBN-13: 978-0-9888713-2-8

To my Heavenly Father: Even when I feel alone, I know You are right there with me. And when I feel like giving up, thank You for giving me the strength to go on. I love You.

To all of the fans of Mona-Lisa, Corey, and Wasif: this one's for you! I hope you enjoy it!

Also by Adrienne Thompson:

Bluesday

Lovely Blues

Been So Long

Little Sister (A Companion Novel to Been So Long)

Rapture (A Been So Long Prequel)

See Me

When You've Been Blessed (Feels Like Heaven)

Coming Soon:

Blues In The Key Of B (Bluesday Book III)

Ain't Nobody

Your Love Is King

Love cannot be drowned by oceans or floods...

Song of Songs 8:7 CEV

Soundtrack provided by Ms. Anita Baker

"Rhythm Of Love"

"Watch Your Step"

"More Than You Know"

"Lately"

"Good Enough"

"Lonely"

"Sometimes"

"Been So Long"

"No One To Blame"

"Just Because"

"Body And Soul"

"Perfect Love Affair"

"Baby"

"Do You Believe Me"

"Squeeze Me"

"No One In The World"

"Caught Up In The Rapture"

"How Could You"

"You're My Everything-Revisited"

"In My Heart"

Soundtrack Continued

"Priceless"

"Lead Me Into Love"

"Feel The Need"

Chapter 1

"Rhythm Of Love"

Corey wrapped his arm around my waist and pulled me closer to him. I purred as I snuggled close to his body. I nuzzled his neck, breathing in his heavenly natural scent. I loved my husband of three years more with each day. I loved him for the man he was and for the way that he loved me—unconditionally and passionately. I smiled as he rubbed his hand up and down my back. I wrapped my arms around his hard, muscular body and sighed. He felt *so good*.

He kissed me softly and whispered, "What you doing awake this time of night?"

I kissed him back and said, "I was just about to ask you the same thing. You're the one with work in the morning."

He pushed my hair from my forehead and kissed it, then my nose, and then my lips again. "Well, I was thinking about putting in a little work right here and right now."

"Mm, my favorite kind of work."

He smiled at me and then began to sing—and I use that term very loosely—an interesting version of Anita Baker's "Good Love".

I returned his smile. "Oh, you're serenading me? You know what that does to me, baby." I kissed him slowly as I ran my hand up and down his arm.

"Just trying to get you in the mood," he said against my lips.

"Baby, I am *always* in the mood for you."

"I'm so glad God made you for me," he whispered.

As thunder rumbled outside and lightning flashed behind the mini blinds on our bedroom window, he began to trail kisses from my mouth, to my neck, to my chest, to my—

Knock, knock.

Corey froze and I sighed. I had no doubt that the soft rapping at our door was from Sahib, my three year-old son, who was deathly afraid of thunderstorms. A bark from my poodle, Lizzie, who'd been sleeping with Sahib since he was a year old, confirmed my suspicions. I had hoped that Sahib would sleep through Mother Nature's light show, but I was sure the booming thunder had awakened him. Corey released a soft groan as he left our bed and opened the door. He picked the pajama-clad toddler up and kissed his cheek.

"What's wrong, little man?" he asked.

Sahib wrapped his arms around Corey's thick neck and rested his head on Corey's shoulder. "I'm scared," he said in a tiny voice.

Corey hugged Sahib. "Aw, remember what I told you? There's nothing to be scared of, right? God will protect you."

Sahib nodded against Corey's shoulder and said, "Yeah, but I'm still scared."

"Well, you wanna sleep in here with me and your mama?"

Sahib nodded his answer and Corey set him in the bed right between us. Sahib quickly scooted over until his body touched mine. I pulled him close to me and kissed his forehead. As I rubbed my fingers through his thick hair, I looked at Corey and mouthed, "I'm sorry."

Corey mouthed, "It's okay."

He wrapped his arm around both me and Sahib and soon all of us were fast asleep, including Lizzie, who'd curled up at the foot of the bed.

***

I began to clear the kitchen table of dishes as the three men in my house—my husband and my 17-year-old twin sons—rushed around, preparing for school and work. Only Sahib was left at the table playing with a bowl of mushy cereal. One by one Corey and the twins, Blair and Morgan, kissed me on the cheek, told me they loved me, and bounced out the door, leaving me and Sahib to face the day together.

The morning flew by as I bathed and dressed Sahib, cleaned the house, played with him, and fed him lunch. I was putting him down for a nap when I heard the doorbell. I didn't even have to check it or wonder who it was. I knew it was Sahib's father, my ex, Wasif. I knew because he always popped up unannounced on Mondays, the one day he knew Corey wouldn't be coming home for lunch since he had lunch duty at the private school where he worked.

I sighed as I slowly walked to the door and unlocked it. I opened it to find Wasif standing before me with a slight smile on his face, his thin frame covered in seal blue scrubs.

"Hey," he said softly.

"Hi," I said as I backed out of the doorway, allowing him into the house.

As usual, he eyed his surroundings, taking in my modest home— a stark contrast to the home I once lived in, the one he'd provided for me, but Corey refused to live in. "Um, how've you been?" he asked as if it hadn't only been a week since he last saw me.

"Great," I said. "I just put Sahib down for a nap. You can peek in on him if you want."

Wasif nodded and headed down the hall to Sahib's room. I went back into the kitchen where I downed a glass of water and then stood staring out the window which was just over the sink. As always, I would be more than glad when Wasif left. I really didn't like the way he always made sure to visit when Corey was gone. It seemed disrespectful to me. And I knew that it bothered Corey.

I was still standing at the window, deep in thought, when I heard Wasif clear his throat. I turned around and saw him leaning against the door facing. "He's out like a light," he said.

"Yeah, well, it's his nap time, but then again, you knew that," I said in a less-than-friendly tone.

He fixed his eyes on me. He looked at me in that way that always made me feel a little weird. When we split up, he declared there would be no reconciling and he'd even gone back to his wife. But his eyes, they said otherwise. His eyes told me he still loved me.

"It's the only time I could get away," he said with a shrug.

I nodded as I dropped my gaze. "Yeah."

We both stood there in the usual awkward silence. Neither of us knew what to say or do next. Even after three years, we both seemed uncertain as to how to interact with one another.

Wasif finally broke the silence with, "Well, I should be going. I'll try to get back over when all three boys are home. Goodbye, Mo."

I walked him to the door. "Bye."

"Oh, almost forgot," he added as he turned around and handed me a check.

"Thanks," I said and watched him leave.

I walked back into the house with the check in my hand and sighed. I slumped into a kitchen chair and stared at the check. It was a lot of money—it was *always* a lot of money. Child support for all three boys—the two he'd fathered and the one whom he'd raised as his own for so many years, though he was actually Corey's son. I laid the check on the table and closed my eyes. The next day, I'd deposit the money into my savings account, where it would stay because Corey refused to accept any of it even as he struggled to pay our bills.

Chapter 2

"Watch Your Step"

I rolled over in bed and reached for Corey, but only felt the cold sheets. I opened my eyes to find his side of the bed empty. My eyes probed the room but I couldn't find him in the darkness. I left our bed and quietly walked through the house until I found him at the kitchen table with envelopes and papers strewn in front of him— bills. I sighed as I took a seat across from him at the table.

He looked up at me and smiled. "Hey, baby," he said softly and then turned his attention back to the bills he'd been studying.

"Hey," I said.

I sat and watched him pour over the bills for ten minutes, and then I said, "Come back to bed."

"Um, I will in just a minute," he said absently. His eyes were glued to a piece of paper.

"Things not adding up? I still have the money—"

"You already know I'm not taking that money, Mona. Don't go

there tonight," he said without looking up from the table.

"Corey, what kind of sense does it make for you to stress over these bills when I have all that money in my savings? Come on, now. You're just being stubborn."

"Mona, *no*. Look, things are just tight this month because we had to get your truck fixed. We'll be ok."

"I can pick up some more days at work." I worked twice a week at the local library.

"No."

"Corey—"

"No!" he said, raising his voice.

I stared at him for a moment before standing from the table and turning to leave the kitchen without a word.

"Baby, wait. I'm...I'm sorry. Come here," he said.

I walked over to him and he pulled me onto his lap and kissed me. "I'm sorry. I didn't mean to raise my voice. Just let me do this, okay? Let me be the man of the house."

"Baby, you *are* the man of the house. I just hate to see you stressing like this. I just wanna help you."

He smiled and kissed the tip of my nose. "I'm not stressing. I'm analyzing. Can't pay bills if I don't know what I'm paying." He planted a long, slow kiss on my lips and added, "Now, let me tuck you in. It's getting late."

I grinned. "Tuck me in? I like the sound of that."

Corey held me close and kissed me for a long, long time. We were just about to do some "tucking in" right there at the kitchen table when we were jolted by the sound of the front door slamming shut. We stared at each other, both wondering who in the world had just come into our home.

Our mutual question was answered when our son, Morgan, came stumbling into the kitchen.

Corey frowned. "You just making it home, Morg?"

Morgan jumped and looked up at us. "Aw, dang. I didn't even see y'all over there. Yeah, I was at the library studying and I guess I lost track of time," he slurred. He walked across the kitchen and snatched the refrigerator door open. "What we got to eat? I'm hungry as a hostage."

"The library closed hours ago, Morgan," I said. I stood from Corey's lap and walked over to Morgan. I grabbed his arm and turned him towards me, getting a nose full of the remnants of marijuana smoke in the process. "You been smoking weed, boy?"

Morgan looked at me and smiled. "Heeeeey, Mama. What's up?"

I could feel Corey standing behind me. "Answer your mother, Morgan."

"Heeeey, Coach Bio Dad." Morgan said and then broke into a loud boisterous laugh. "Bio Dad—sounds like a sad-ass super hero." More laughter.

"He acts like he's been smoking more than weed. And he's probably drunk, too," Corey said.

I grabbed his shirt collar and shook him. "Morgan! Morgan, what have you been smoking?"

Morgan smiled at me. "Hmmmm? Smoking? I dunno." He shrugged and snorted out another laugh.

Corey grabbed his arm and began to steer him out of the kitchen. "Come on, son. Let's get you to bed. We'll talk about this in the morning."

Morgan gave Corey a sloppy salute and said, "Yessir, coach!" His laughter seemed to grow louder and louder as Corey led him down the short hallway to the bedroom he shared with his brother, Blair. I followed them and watched as Morgan climbed into his bed while singing a garbled version of a Keyshia Cole song. I looked over at Blair who was sitting up on the side of his bed with a concerned look on his face.

"You got any idea what he's on?" I asked Blair.

Blair shrugged. "No, I wasn't with him. We don't hang out much anymore."

I frowned slightly. "Really? Why?"

"I don't know. We just don't."

Corey walked back over to me and grabbed my hand. "Let's go to bed." He turned to Blair and added, "Goodnight, Blair."

"Goodnight, Coach," Blair said before falling back onto his pillow.

Corey and I climbed into our bed but I found it impossible to sleep. What was going on with our son?

***

I held a sleeping Sahib in my lap as I mulled over the events of the previous night. I was very disturbed by Morgan's behavior. I was eager to confront him, but he'd managed to slip out of the house before either Corey or I woke up. I was worried about him.

For the first 14 years of my twins' lives, I had believed they were both Wasif's sons. It wasn't until three years ago that I realized that Morgan was, in fact, Corey's son. Morgan and Blair had taken the news remarkably well—or so I thought. Too well, I guess. Now it seemed that Morgan was having a delayed reaction, or was it something else? Why would he be experimenting with drugs at this point in his life, when his future was so bright.

Both Blair and Morgan were being courted by several NCAA colleges due to their extraordinary basketball talent. They were almost assured a full ride to the college of their choice. Why would Morgan do something to mess that up?

I put my thoughts on hold to answer the ringing telephone. "Hello?"

"Good afternoon, Mo."

I smiled at hearing my younger sister's voice. We'd only reconnected a few years earlier, but it felt like we'd never been apart. "Hey, Cleo. So glad you called." She was "Gina" now, but she'd always be Cleo to me.

"Why? What's up?"

I told her about the most recent events of my life—everything from Corey's stubbornness to Morgan's disturbing behavior. To which she replied, "I'm gonna pray for you."

"I sure need it," I said.

"Seriously, Corey's just the textbook version of an alpha-male. But you already knew that and I'm sure that's one of the things you love about him. He and Scott are a lot alike. Just let him do his thing and stop worrying." Scott was Cleo's husband.

"Yeah, you're right." And she *was* right. With Wasif, it was easy for me to get my way. Actually, if I said it—Wasif did it. With Corey, things were totally different. He loved me, but he'd never just go along with whatever I wanted. He was definitely his own man.

"And as for Morgan, you just need to talk to him. He's at that weird age, you know? He reminds me of my Aaron. He just needs some guidance. But he also needs space. Don't pressure him too much. You do need to get to the bottom of this drug thing, but remember, he's a good kid. Things haven't been easy for him or Blair." Aaron was Cleo's oldest son.

"Yeah, you're right again. You're just so smart, Sis. Thanks."

"Life has taught me well—too well. I know people, *especially* men."

"Yeah," I said softly. I hated thinking of the things Cleo endured after she ran away from home. She'd definitely learned a lot about people and life—more than anyone should have to know.

"How's Aaron doing?" I asked. Aaron had been through a very traumatic experience with his biological father only a couple of years earlier.

"The same. He's just really quiet most of the time. And when he does talk, he refuses to discuss the incident. It's like he's trying to act as if it never happened."

"Yeah, I know how that is. There were a lot of things I tried to convince myself never happened."

"Yeah, me too."

"Um, have you given any more thought to what your counselor suggested?" I asked after a moment of mutual silence.

"You mean visiting Mama?"

"Yeah."

Cleo sighed. "I think about it all the time. I'm just not ready. I'm not sure I can handle going back there."

"I understand. It wasn't easy for me, either."

"Yeah, and every time I think I can do it, something comes to mind—a memory—that makes me reconsider."

"I understand that, too. There are so many memories…" I stared across the room at nothing in particular.

"You know what I thought about the other day?" Cleo asked.

"No, what?"

"My seventh birthday. You remember that?"

My grip on the phone tightened. I did remember it—too well.

"Yes, I do," I said, my voice barely above a whisper.

"It was unforgettable, wasn't it?"

"Cleo—"

"Look, Mo. I gotta go. Tell Corey and the boys I said hi. Love you. Bye."

"Okay, tell Scott and the kids I said hello. Love you, too. Bye, Cleo."

I laid my phone down and sighed as the memories of that day so long ago rushed to my mind. I was eleven and Cleo was seven. Up until that year, our grandmother had been good about baking us a birthday cake and giving us at least one gift. It was usually some cheap dollar store doll or plastic tea set, but it was more than our mother had ever bought us, so we were always excited and thankful.

But that year, our mother and grandmother got into a big argument a few days before Cleo's birthday. It went like most of their arguments, starting with our grandmother chiding our mother for being unfit and ending with our mother calling our grandmother a series of less-than-complimentary names, all of them beginning with the word "white". White witch, white cow, white tramp—and so on. And when she really wanted to get under Grandma's skin, she addressed her by her first name—Patty.

On the day of her seventh birthday, Cleo made the mistake of asking when "Granny" was coming with her cake and gift. What followed is forever engrained in my mind.

Mama looked up at Cleo and rolled her eyes. "That witch ain't welcome here no more. Now go watch TV or something."

Cleo just stood there, her round eyes filling with tears. I knew if she didn't move Mama would light into her for being disobedient. I walked over to her and grabbed her hand.

"Come on, Cleo," I said softly.

But Cleo didn't budge. Maybe she was in shock or something or maybe she was just a little girl who wanted a birthday cake and a toy. Whatever the reason, she stood her ground.

"Cleo," I repeated. I pulled on her hand but she snatched away.

She stood there and stared at Mama, whose eyes changed in an instant.

"Cleo," I said again. I knew what was coming, and I'd do anything to prevent it.

"Did you hear me, little girl? Go watch TV!" Mama shrieked. She could go from zero to one-hundred in a second flat.

"I want Grandma," Cleo said softly. "Can I call her?"

"Call her?" Mama said as if it was the most absurd thing she'd ever heard.

Cleo nodded.

*"Call her? What? You think I'm lying? Get out of my house!!"
Mama screamed, bolting from her seat. Now she was in Cleo's face.*

Cleo and I both jumped back.

"Mama—" I began.

"Shut up, Mo!" Mama snapped.

*I backed away from her, pulling on Cleo's hand, urging her to
follow suit. She stumbled backward but Mama grabbed her by the
arm and pulled her back to her.*

"You going the wrong way! I said, get outta my house! Now!"

*Mama dragged Cleo to the front door and shoved her outside into
the frigid January air with Cleo wearing only a t-shirt and jeans.
Mama locked the door behind her.*

I stood in the middle of the living room floor, staring at the door.

*Mama reclaimed her seat on the couch and lit a cigarette. She
turned to me and said, "Don't even think about letting her back in.
Try it and you gon' be out there with her."*

*Tears flooded my eyes. My heart ached as I stood there and
listened to Cleo bang on the door and beg to come back in. "It's
cold out here, Mama!" she screamed through the door.*

I wanted to let her in, but more than that, I wanted to hurt my mother for putting her out. I truly hated her. I walked to the door, opened it, and walked outside in my bare feet. I grabbed my little sister and held her close to me as the door swung shut behind me. The sound of our mother locking the door sent more of a chill through me than the cold wind that was howling around us.

We huddled on the landing next to our apartment door for a long time, teeth chattering, bodies trembling. Cleo buried her head in my chest, her warm tears wetting the thin fabric of my blouse. I rubbed my hands up and down her back, trying to warm her, but how could I? I was freezing, myself. Neighbors walked by and gave us curious looks, but not one of them lifted a finger to help us. No one called child services or the police. I hated them. I hated my mother.

We'd been out there for most of the day and the sun was beginning to set when I heard the lock turn in the door. I waited for it to open, but it didn't. I waited for as long as I could, but my feet and hands were growing numb and Cleo was having a hard time staying awake, so I cautiously opened the door and peered inside.

"Come in if you coming in, and close the damn door. You letting all the heat out," Mama barked from her seat on the couch.

I inched into the apartment, nearly dragging my frozen sister behind me. We went straight to bed, burrowing underneath the covers without any thought of lunch or dinner—neither of which we'd eaten. I snuggled close to Cleo, trying to transfer what little body heat I had left to her.

I kissed her forehead and whispered, "Happy birthday, Cleo."

She answered me with a soft snore.

As I sat there wiping the tears brought on by the memory, I felt a new sadness for Cleo. She'd survived a lot of horrible things and she knew all about abuse and healing. She had a good husband and wonderful children. And in marrying Scott, she'd inherited a large extended family who welcomed her with open arms. Yet, in the midst of all that, she still held on to those terrible memories of our childhood. So did I. Time hadn't done a very good job of healing either of our wounds.

I stood to take Sahib into his bedroom when I heard a knock at the door. It was only 11:30 am—too early for Corey to be home for lunch and besides, he had a key. Why would he be knocking? I laid Sahib on the couch and headed to the door. "Who is it?!" I called.

"Mona, open the door!" It *was* Corey.

I snatched the door open to find Corey with one hand on Morgan's arm and the other holding Morgan's backpack. Morgan stood before me with a dejected and rather embarrassed look on his face.

"I found him," Corey said.

I cleared the doorway for them to enter. Corey pulled Morgan into the house. Morgan squinted at me as he stumbled inside. Corey dropped the backpack on the floor and it landed with a thud. Corey's expression was a mixture of exhaustion and disappointment. I'd felt him tossing and turning most of the night.

"Corey, you've been looking for Morgan? I thought you went to work?" I asked, looking from him to Morgan.

"I was at work when I found him. One of the other students saw him sleeping in the backseat of his car on the parking lot."

I frowned. "Morgan, what in the world is wrong with you?"

Morgan grimaced and grasped his forehead. "Hey, hey, why you hollering at me? My head hurts."

I stepped closer to him. "Good. I'm glad your head is hurting. Maybe you'll think twice before you get high or drunk again. Now, what the hell is wrong with you? Coming up in here last night disrespecting me and your father?! And then you have the nerve to sneak out of the house this morning?" I was more relieved that he was okay than mad. But I needed to know what was going on with him.

Morgan rolled his eyes. "Which father?" *That* hurt.

"Morg—" Corey began, but I interrupted him.

"Is that your problem?" I asked.

Morgan scoffed, "Among other things."

"Like what?" I said.

"Everything," he said with a shrug.

"Look, Morgan, I told you we could talk about Corey being your father. I even offered to take both you and Blair to counseling but you said everything was okay. You said you were okay with Corey being your dad. You said you liked having a father full time. Now this? All these years later?"

"Look, I'm going through some things right now and this fake family of ours is getting on my nerves."

"Fake?" Corey chimed in. "Son, I love you boys and I love your mother. We might not be a perfect family, but we're a *real* family. We talked about this before, remember?"

Morgan sighed. "Look, folks. I got a lot on my mind right now. I don't have time for this."

"What's on your mind, Morgan? You can talk to us about anything," Corey said.

Morgan leaned against the wall of the foyer and shoved his hands into his pockets. I knew him well enough to know that he was shutting down. He was done talking to us.

"Well, would you prefer talking to your dad, Wasif?" I asked. From the corner of my eye, I could see Corey's expression change.

Morgan looked up at me and shook his head. "I'm fine, Ma. Sorry for the way I acted last night. Won't happen again." With that, he grabbed his backpack and headed towards his bedroom.

"We're not done here, Morgan," Corey called after him.

I laid my hand on Corey's arm and said, "Let him go, baby. It's alright."

Corey snatched away from me. "He's my son, too, Mona-Lisa. And I'm not done talking to him."

I watched as Corey headed down the hall behind Morgan. I walked into the living room and released a frustrated sigh. I'd upset him by bringing up Wasif. If Corey had his way, Wasif would've disappeared from the face of the earth by now. He despised him—blamed him for keeping Morgan away from him for so many years.

I looked over at Sahib as he slept peacefully. Just when I thought things were going well, they always seemed to unravel.

Chapter 3

"More Than You Know"

The remainder of that evening was quiet, dinner was strained, and lying in that bed next to Corey was akin to sleeping with a rock. So I tucked my tail and decided to go for a truce.

I rolled over and faced his back. I lifted his t-shirt and gently kissed his shoulder. "I'm sorry if I upset you," I whispered.

Corey didn't move or answer me.

"And I'm willing to work hard to make it up to you," I said as I gently rubbed his huge arm.

Still no response.

I snuggled closely behind him. "I love you, Coach Sanders," I whispered as I kissed his back. "I love you so much."

I could feel Corey relax and a few seconds later, he turned over and faced me. "I love you, too, Mona," he said then kissed me.

"You forgive me?"

He nodded. "Yeah and I shouldn't have overreacted. It's just that sometimes I feel like a fifth wheel in this family. Like Wasif's the real dad and I'm some type of replacement."

I looked him in the eye, taking in all of his hurt and frustration. "Baby, Wasif isn't half the man you are. You stepped up and became a better father to those boys than Wasif could ever be. You are here with them each and every day. You love them and they love you. But I can't act like Wasif doesn't exist. He's still a part of their lives which makes him a part of *our* lives, if only a small part."

"I know. It's just something I have to deal with. Me and God. I'll be okay."

I smiled. "I know you will. Did you get anywhere with Morgan?"

"Nah, he's stubborn just like his mama. Wouldn't talk to me."

"I ain't the only one of his parents who's stubborn," I muttered.

"What was that?" he asked with raised eyebrows.

"Nothing. He'll come around. He's got a good head on his shoulders, like his father. He just needs a little time."

Corey nodded. "Yeah, I know."

"Corey, you wanna talk about having another baby?"

"No, we've already discussed this. Every pregnancy you've had has had complications. I'm not gonna put you through that again. I love you too much for that."

"But—"

"No buts." He gently rubbed his hand up and down my back. "Now, what was that about you making it up to me? I seem to recall something about you being willing to put in some hard work?"

"Mmhmm. I sure am, but first I want you in my favorite uniform."

Corey planted a long kiss on my lips and said, "No problem."

I watched as he stood from the bed and stripped out of his clothes—*all* of his clothes. Then he walked over to the closet and draped his coach's whistle around his neck.

"How's this?" he asked as he climbed back into the bed.

I pulled him close to me and said, "Mm, you know how I love a man in uniform."

***

The next morning, we had a much more cordial breakfast as a family than the previous night's dinner, even if Corey spent most of it pouring over the bills again. As I climbed into my vehicle and made my way to the daycare, I prayed that Corey would stop being so stubborn, but I knew better. He'd have rather worked seven jobs than take a dime of Wasif's money.

I dropped Sahib off and headed to the library for my day's work. As I drove, I punched a birth control pill out of the pouch and grabbed my bottled water, but instead of downing the pill like I did every morning, I hesitated. I laid the pill down and after I pulled onto the library parking lot, I sat in my car and punched the rest of the pills out of the pack and tossed them into a plastic sack I found on the floor of the car. As I entered the building, I pitched the sack in a trash can.

I didn't need Corey's permission to give him a baby. I owed it to him. He deserved to raise a baby of his own. And if I had anything to do with it, he'd do just that.

Chapter 4

"Lately"

Another Monday and another visit from Wasif. I gave him a strained smile as I let him into the house. I really wished he'd stop showing up when Corey wasn't home. But that was a wasted wish. I knew he would continue to avoid Corey like the plague, even though it meant him missing Blair and Morgan as well. At least he managed to arrive before Sahib's nap this time. I don't think he'd seen him with his eyes open in weeks.

I left them alone in the living room, headed into the kitchen, and sat at the table where our bills were neatly stacked. Studying those bills had become a daily ritual for Corey and as Wasif entered the kitchen and handed me yet another check, I sighed.

"Thanks," I said and laid the check on the table.

"Sure," He said and smiled at me. He looked me in the eye for a moment and then we both dropped our gazes. "Um, Sahib's getting big, and he's so smart."

I nodded. "Yeah, he's growing really fast. And he is very smart. Just—" I cut myself off. I was going to say "just like his father", but it felt wrong. It was crazy that I felt so awkward around a man I used to love so much.

Wasif jangled his car keys in his hand and cleared his throat. "Um, well, I better be going. Tell Blair and Morgan I'll try to get by later this week to see them."

He always said that, but it never happened. Instead of saying "Okay" like I usually did, I said, "Wasif, Morgan's been acting out lately. I think he might even be experimenting with drugs."

"What?!" he said with a look of alarm on his face.

I nodded. "I know. It really concerns me. You think you could talk to him? He really needs it."

Wasif nodded. "Of course. Thanks for telling me."

"No problem. You're still his father."

He smiled again. "I'll call you after I talk to him. Bye, Mo."

"Bye."

***

Corey made it home a little earlier than usual that evening. He presented me with a bouquet of pale pink roses and announced that we were going out for dinner—just him and me. Morgan was nowhere to be found, but Blair had agreed to babysit Sahib for us. After much primping, we headed out to one of my favorite restaurants where I ordered the shrimp feast, Corey had the porterhouse steak, and we shared a bottle of rather expensive wine. All the while, I wondered what had brought on this treat. I was in the middle of enjoying a velvety slice of chocolate cheesecake when my question was answered.

"You enjoying the evening so far, baby?" Corey asked as he reached across the table for my hand.

So far? What else did he have planned? I nodded my head and smiled. "I am. To what do I owe this treat?"

He smiled nervously. "Well, you deserve this and more for being the best wife in the world."

I grinned. "Aw, thanks, baby."

"And...uh...um, I wanted to discuss something with you. Something I've been thinking about. I wanted to run it by you and see what you think."

I leaned back in my chair. I had a feeling I wasn't going to like whatever Corey was about to say. Why else would he have wined and dined me first? He was trying to soften the blow.

Corey's eyes were fixed on the table as his rubbed his thumb across the top of my hand as he often did. He sucked in a deep breath and slowly released it. It seemed he was purposely prolonging his revelation.

"Um, you know things are not the best for us financially, right?" he finally said.

I tilted my head to one side and said, "It doesn't have to be that way. If only you'd let me—"

Corey released an exasperated sigh. "Come on, Mona. You already know I'm not taking that money."

I loosened my hand from his grip and folded my arms across my chest. "Yeah, well, I don't understand why. It's called *child support* for a reason."

"Look, Dr. Masood's paying the twins' school tuition and that's enough. Plus, he bought them both cars against my wishes. It's *my* job to support this family. Anyway, I've figured out a way that money won't be an issue anymore. Will you let me tell you?"

I closed my eyes and pursed my lips. "Fine. Go ahead."

"I'm thinking seriously about enlisting in the Air Force again."

I sat there and stared at him and thought to myself that I must've been losing my mind because I couldn't have heard what I thought I heard. "What?" I asked. I was tempted to stick a finger in my ear and jiggle it around a little bit just to be sure it was working properly.

He leaned forward and reached for my hands but I didn't move a muscle. I had to be sure I was hearing him right and I was afraid that if I moved, my hearing would be distorted again.

He clasped his hands and said, "I said, I'm thinking about enlisting in the Air Force again." Yep. I'd heard him correctly. Then he droned on and on about how great an opportunity this was and how great the benefits were and what an honor it would be to serve his country again. And I just stared at him like he was a fool, because that's what he sounded like to me—a fool.

"Well, what do you think? I really want to know how you feel about this, Mona," he said, finishing his little spiel.

I was silent for a moment and from the look on Corey's face, my silence was uncomfortable. Finally I said, "So you've really been thinking about this, huh?"

He cleared his throat and his eyes searched mine. "Well, yes, I have."

"Mmhmm, and did you think about which divorce lawyer you're going to retain. Because if you actually do this, you'll need one."

His mouth dropped open and he fell against the back of his chair as if my words had literally hit him. "Baby—"

"Baby, nothing!" I said and stood from the table. I grabbed my purse and stormed out of the restaurant. I dug in my purse for my set of keys to Corey's truck as I walked across the parking lot only to find that I'd left them at home. *Damn!* I thought. Now I'd have to wait for him to drive me home. I leaned against the passenger door and waited for about five minutes before Corey finally emerged from the restaurant, a bewildered look on his face. He opened my door for me and I climbed in without a word. I could feel him glancing at me during the drive home, but I kept my eyes straight ahead.

Had he lost his mind? Did he really think I'd go along with this? Surely not. Surely he knew me better than that! I was not going to go along with being away from my husband for weeks or months at a time. And God forbid if they sent him off to some hostile country. What would I do if something happened to him? I didn't even want to think about it. I love the old USA, but I damn sure wasn't willing to sacrifice my happiness for it. That kind of selflessness just wasn't in my DNA.

Back home, I checked on the boys, took a shower, and dressed for bed without so much as a grunt in Corey's direction. At bedtime, I climbed into the bed and scooted as close to the edge as I could manage without falling off. With my back to him, I could hear him sighing and rustling paper and mumbling—all failed attempts to get my attention.

I'd almost drifted off to sleep when I heard his voice. "Baby, you sleep?" he asked.

I opened my eyes, poised to say something sarcastic in rebuttal, but the sight before me made me swallow my words. Standing before me was my big tall husband wearing nothing but a baseball cap. I leaned up on one arm and eyed him for a moment because even in my anger, I had to admit that the man was fine.

I cleared my throat. "What are you doing?" I asked.

"I'm wearing your favorite uniform," he said as he kneeled beside the bed.

I shook my head. "No, my favorite uniform includes a whistle, remember?"

He smiled. "Well, I thought I'd try something different. You know, spice things up a bit?"

"I see. And you think that I'll forget about your plans just because you're naked?"

"There are no plans if you're not on board with me. I told you I wanted to get your opinion on it. You're everything to me, Mona. If you don't want me to do it, just say the word."

"Word."

He leaned in and kissed me. "Then that settles it. Now, for the best part about fighting."

"Mm, what's that?"

"Making up."

Chapter 5

"Good Enough"

To my surprise, Wasif didn't show up for a visit the following Monday. Instead, he called.

"Hey, I'm not gonna make it today. I'm covering for my partner and it looks like I'm gonna be busy all day. Sorry." Wasif had sold his part of his old practice to his father and had started a new one with an old med school buddy. They were doing very well.

"It's...it's okay," I said, not sure what else to say.

"Okay, well tell Sahib I'll try to see him later this week."

"Okay."

"Oh, and I talked to Morgan. He's just dealing with some guy stuff. He'll be okay. He promised not to mess around with any drugs again and he swears it was only marijuana."

"I'm still worried. I mean, marijuana is a drug."

"I know, but all in all Morgan is a good kid. I'm gonna talk to him more often and keep a closer check on him. He'll be fine, Mo."

"Oh, okay. Thanks for talking to him."

"No problem. He's still my son, right?"

"Right."

We hung up and I just sat there at the kitchen table feeling lost. Though I hated for Wasif to show up when Corey wasn't home, I had to admit that it was now a part of my routine. I was kind of disappointed that he wasn't coming. I stared at nothing in particular, disturbed by my own feelings and wondered why I suddenly felt so hollow inside. As I sat there I fully realized that I was missing Wasif. What was that about? I loved Corey Sanders with everything inside of me. He loved me, too. I knew that beyond the shadow of a doubt. He showed me in every way. So why in the world was I so crestfallen at the thought of not seeing Wasif?

***

Corey brought me flowers again that evening. Of course I was suspicious of his motives. What idea had he cooked up now? This time, we stayed home and I cooked dinner. I was happy to see Morgan at the table with the rest of our family. He'd been pulling rather frequent disappearing acts, and though I was really trying to give him space, I was worried about him.

Thankfully, he was his old self as he sat there having a lively conversation with Corey and Blair. He even held Sahib in his lap and shared some ice cream with him during dessert. I felt a sense of relief and hoped that his improved behavior wasn't temporary.

After dinner, the boys headed into the living room and played video games. Corey stayed behind and helped me clean the table and wash the dishes.

"How was your day, baby?" he asked as I handed him a plate to rinse and dry.

"Okay," I said, trying to mask the disturbing disappointment that lingered.

"Just okay?" Corey prodded. "Did Dr. Masood come by to see Sahib?"

I shook my head, careful to keep my eyes on the soapy dish water. "No, he didn't."

"Oh really? Well, anyway, I have some exciting news," he said brightly.

Here we go, I thought. "Yeah, what's that?" I asked as I dipped the dish towel in the water and began to wash a plate.

"You know how people are always asking me about my workout

regimen?"

I glanced up at him and saw that he looked excited instead of apprehensive. I stopped washing dishes and said, "Yeah and I can see why." I looked him up and down and he chuckled.

"Well, a couple of the guys at work have asked me about being their personal trainer. It would only be a couple of evenings a week and maybe a few Saturdays, but they're willing to pay top dollar for me to help them get in shape."

"Wow, really?" I was genuinely surprised. This idea was much better than the Air Force thing.

"Yep. And who knows, this might lead to me starting my own business doing something I love to do anyway. So what do you think?"

I turned to him and hugged him around his waist. "I think you're excited about this, and I'm excited for you."

"So it's okay with you?" he asked as he wrapped his arms around me.

"As long as you promise it'll only be a couple days a week, I'm fine with it."

He released a relieved sigh and kissed the top of my head. "Good. I really am excited about this. I feel like this could really change things for us financially. This could be big, Mona!"

I smiled as I rested my head against his chest. "Oh, and if you happen to get any female customers, you let them know that you are taken."

He kissed my neck and said, "*Very* taken."

I nodded. "Um hmm, and I won't hesitate to slap a witch if she gets out of line."

"Now you know I've only got eyes for you, baby."

"Keep it that way."

Chapter 6

"Lonely"

A few afternoons a week soon turned into *every* afternoon and *every* Saturday. I saw less and less of my husband and I missed him terribly. He usually made it home after bedtime and he even had clients that he met during the early morning hours. We rarely had dinner as a family anymore, the two of us hardly ever talked, and sex had become basically an afterthought, but he was riding high from the success of his new business and I didn't have the heart to rain on his parade by whining about being lonely. Still, I missed him and I felt very alone.

But when he announced that he'd taken off work to attend a week-long personal training seminar in Florida, I just about fell to pieces. I was about to come unhinged as I watched him cheerily pack his bag. I needed him here with me. I needed him, period. He looked up at me and smiled as he whistled a tune, oblivious to the whirlwind of emotions I was experiencing.

After he finished packing, he walked over to me, kissed my cheek, and handed me an obscene roll of money—earnings from his new business. "Here's some spending change," he said proudly. "I'll be back Sunday." He kissed my cheek again and added, "I love you, baby."

"I love you, too. I...I'll miss you," I said softly. Fighting the urge to grab him and never let him go.

He looked me in the eye. "Are you okay, baby? Is something wrong?"

"I..." I stood there for a moment before deciding against asking him to stay. "I just wanted to give you this," I said as I wrapped my arms around him and kissed him slowly.

I felt his hands grip my waist as he returned the kiss. When our kiss ended, he stepped back and said, "Well, thank you."

I rubbed my hand down his chest. "Um, what time does your plane leave?"

"Uh, in a couple of hours. I know what you're thinking and Lord knows I want it, too, but I'll miss my flight."

I gave him a little pout as I nodded. "Okay, well, your loss."

He leaned in and kissed my neck. "Don't I know it? Look, just keep that on ice till I get back."

As sad as I was to see him go, I had to smile at his last statement.

***

I'm not sure what woke me in the middle of the night. When I sat up in the bed, the house was still and quiet. No dreams or nightmares had invaded my rest. I suppose it must've been mother's intuition or something like that because my body seemed to automatically move to a standing position and lead itself down the hall to Sahib's bedroom. I could smell his body heat from the doorway. I rushed across the room and lifted him into my arms. If the fever didn't scare me then the limpness of his body surely did.

In a panic, I ran to the twins' bedroom and flicked on the light. "Boys! Boys! We need to get to the hospital! Sahib is sick!"

Both Blair and Morgan bolted up in bed nearly simultaneously. "You want me to call Coach?" Blair asked groggily.

I turned to leave the room. "Yes and your dad, too."

I ran to my room, laid Sahib on the bed, and quickly stepped into a pair of house shoes before snatching a coat on over my gown. Morgan came into the room still dressed in a t-shirt and his pajama pants and scooped Sahib up from the bed. We headed outside to find Blair behind the wheel of his car waiting for us.

I climbed into the passenger seat and Morgan handed Sahib to me before climbing into the backseat. As Blair raced out of the driveway he said, "Couldn't get Coach. Dad's gonna meet us there."

In the ER, I made sure to mention that Sahib was Dr. Wasif Masood's son, hoping that it would speed up the process for him. It did. Sahib was taken back in almost seconds. I was allowed to go back with him and as I sat next to the bed holding his hot little hand, the walls began to close in around me. How had my little boy, who'd been fine when I put him to bed, gotten so sick so quickly? What was wrong with him? And where in the hell was the doctor?

I was just about to go find one myself when a nurse came in, started an IV, and drew some blood. Then she took his vital signs and left with a promise that the doctor would be in shortly. Well, I guess her idea of shortly differed greatly from mine because, I swear it was at least twenty minutes from the time she left the little cold examining room to the time the door swung back open and a petite female wearing a white lab coat with the name Meredith Graumer, MD stitched on it entered. Behind her was a sight that totally put me at ease. There stood Wasif in his green surgery scrubs, a concerned look on his face.

I leaned against the back of the chair and sighed loudly then I buried my face in my hands and thanked God Wasif was here. *Now* something would be done to help my baby.

"Hi, I'm Dr. Graumer," the lady said in a pleasant voice. I was sure she was trying to put me at ease having seen my harried expression when she opened the door. "Let me see what's going on with this little fella."

Wasif stood to the side and watched as Dr. Graumer donned a pair of gloves and began her examination. Once she was done, she turned to me. "Has he been complaining about any pain?" she asked.

I sat there for a moment and tried to remember if he had, but as far as I could remember, he hadn't.

"Well, it looks like he has some type of virus. There's one going around right now that's especially hard on young children. He might have picked it up at daycare. We're still waiting on blood cultures. They take a little time to complete, but once we have the results we'll know exactly what we're dealing with and how to fight it. In the meantime, I'll order a fever reducer and send him up to Peds for the night."

I thanked her and watched as she left the room. I looked over at Wasif and said, "Thanks so much for being here. I know it made a difference in his care."

Wasif frowned. "Well, I like to think they treat all the patients the same."

I gave him a skeptical look.

Wasif shrugged. "Well, anyway, he's my son. I'm supposed to be here."

I looked up and saw the sincere look on his face and that's when the tears started. I don't know where they came from. I have no idea why I started crying. Maybe it was just the thought of my baby being sick coupled with the fact that my husband was away and maybe the fact that my marriage was not in the best condition had something to do with it. I really don't know, but I do know that when I felt Wasif's hand on my shoulder, I didn't recoil. And when he squatted next to me and pulled me into his arms I didn't resist. I leaned into him and closed my eyes and listened to him promise that our son would be okay. He guaranteed it. And I believed him.

I sent the twins home and spent the night in Sahib's room on a less-than-comfortable chair, watching him and watching the nurses and techs that milled in and out. Wasif spent the night on the opposite side of the bed, asleep in a straight-back chair with his head resting against a window. I watched him, too. I wondered if his wife knew where he was.

I checked my phone obsessively, hoping that Corey would call, but he didn't. I stared at the floor, the walls, the window—anything but sleep.

By the next morning, Sahib's fever had broken, and he was given his first round of IV antibiotics. By noon, he was beginning to perk up a bit, and I felt my body begin to relax. Because of my sleepless night, I also felt fatigue set in. I didn't realize I'd drifted off until I felt someone tapping my shoulder. I opened my eyes to find Wasif standing over me with a cup of something steamy in his hands.

"Coffee?" he asked.

I smiled up at him. Stubble was already beginning to shadow his face and his scrubs looked extra wrinkled. "Thanks," I said.

He nodded wearily as he walked over to his chair and sat down. "You slept through Dr. Graumer's visit. She says he's improving. He can probably go home tomorrow."

I leaned back in my chair and closed my eyes. "Thank God! I was so worried."

"I know. Me, too."

I stared down at the thick coffee then looked over at Sahib who was sound asleep in the hospital bed. "Um, Wasif. I appreciate you for being here, but you don't have to stay tonight. We'll be okay. I know you have your family to think about."

Wasif looked over at me, his brow furrowed. "Sahib *is* my family, Mo. What are you talking about? You must really be tired. What you just said sounds nothing like you."

I sat up straight in my seat. "What is that supposed to mean?"

He eyed me for a moment as if he was trying to decide whether or not to verbalize what was in his mind. Then he said, "I mean that my other family never mattered to you before."

I stared at him for a moment. Sahib might've been sick, but did he really think he could go there with me? "Hell, they still don't. I was just trying to be nice, but forget it. Do what you want, just don't say anything else to me."

"There she is," he said with a smug look on his face. "The woman who threw me away for a damn coach."

I rolled my eyes. "No, dear. I threw a coward away for a hero." With that, I stood to leave. "I'm going down to the cafeteria for a while before I really hurt your feelings."

"Too late," he said.

"Yeah, whatever."

No sooner than I'd made it into the hallway, my cell phone rang. It was Corey. "Hello?" I answered.

"Hey, baby," he said, sounding relieved. "I am so sorry I missed your calls. My phone went dead and I forgot to turn it on after I charged it."

"Mmhmm," I said dryly. I was pretty well pissed off at the world at that point.

"Is Sahib okay? You need me to come back?"

"He's better. And as for your second question, figure the answer out on your own." I ended the call and stalked to the cafeteria. I called Blair and Morgan and gave them an update on Sahib. I didn't have much of an appetite, so after eating an apple and downing a bottle of water, I headed back to Sahib's room where Wasif and I basically ignored each other.

The next morning Sahib was discharged. Wasif left the hospital, and Corey arrived shortly before we left for home.

Chapter 7

"Sometimes"

I didn't speak to Corey for three days—punishment for being away when Sahib got sick or for going away at all, I guess. I don't really know, but his misery made me feel better. When Wasif came by on Monday, I simply opened the door and walked back to my room. I didn't look at him or smile. I didn't bother speaking or telling him where Sahib was. My house was small enough that I figured he'd find him. And there was no sense in pretending with niceties. He'd made it clear how he felt about me in that hospital room—he was still angry and hurt about our breakup. I didn't care, though.

I was sitting on the side of my bed reading a book when I heard the soft knock. I looked up at Wasif who stood in the doorway with his hands in the pockets of his slacks, his eyes downcast.

He sighed heavily. "Look, I'm sorry for what I said the other night. It was not the right time or the right thing to say in that situation."

I stared at him for a moment and then returned my attention to my book.

"Mo, we've got to have some type of relationship for the boys' sake."

I stood and walked towards the door, sliding past him. I could hear him following me as I made my destination—the front door. I opened it and stepped to the side.

He stood in front of me. "So this is what it's going to be like from now on? You're gonna keep giving me the silent treatment? Did what I said really upset you that much?"

I raised my eyes to meet his. "No, but I don't have time for whining and complaining from grown men, that's all."

He backed up a little. "Whining and complaining? Wow, you really are a cold-hearted woman. Forget it, I prefer the silent treatment."

"Good."

He stepped toward the door and hesitated. "You know, Mo. I wish I knew what about Corey Sanders made it so easy for you to throw me away. I wonder about that all the time."

I sighed. "Well, I guess it's the same reason you married another woman and made me your mistress."

He turned and looked me in the eye. "I've apologized for that. I tried to make up for it. I left her, remember? My father has barely spoken to me in years."

"And that's my fault? *You* made those decisions. You made *all* of those decisions—including marrying that woman! And anyway, you went right back to her. You don't get brownie points for leaving and going back!" I said, raising my voice.

His shoulders sagged. "Mo…look, I didn't mean for this to be an argument. I…I just wanted you to understand."

I placed my hands on my hips and leaned forward. "Understand what, Wasif? What the hell are you talking about?"

"That…" he paused, a pensive look on his face.

"What?" I asked, my patience running thin.

"Nothing. I gotta go. I'll be back next week."

I shrugged. "Fine. Whatever."

I closed the door and leaned against it, wondering why after three years, we were rehashing the past and why did it make me feel so bad?

***

Corey made it home right after work at the school. He'd been doing that every day since his return from the conference. I guess it finally occurred to him that his constant absence was a problem. I was still upset, but my earlier exchange with Wasif had removed most of my anger from Corey and directed it towards Wasif. So when he made it home, I spoke to him, even kissed him on the cheek.

Dinner was uneventful and when we went to bed, I didn't resist when he snuggled close to me and wrapped his arms around me. He was a good man with misguided motives. He was trying to prove that he could be as good a caregiver to me and the boys as Wasif. I knew that was his mission. I just wished I could make him understand that none of that mattered to me. He'd loved me, married me, and was now raising two kids that weren't even his. He was good to me in many ways. That's what mattered to me.

As I lay there in his arms, I realized that maybe I wasn't doing enough to make him understand. I needed to show him and to tell him. So I did.

I rubbed my hand over his and said, "I love you."

"I love you, too."

"And I appreciate you for all you do."

He kissed the back of my head. "I appreciate you, too."

"Then will you let me work an extra day at the library so that you can be home more? I miss you."

He was quiet for a moment as if mulling over my proposition. "No, I just can't do that, baby. I need to take care of you, and I need you to understand that. I'll cut back and try to be home more, though."

I guessed that was a good as it was going to get. So when he reached over and pulled me towards him, I said, "Okay."

Chapter 8

"Been So Long"

"What's going on with your family?" I asked as I balanced the phone on my shoulder and placed a plate in front of Sahib. I smiled as his face lit up. Chicken fingers were his favorite.

"Same old thing. Work, trying to balance the kids' busy schedules, tending to my hubby," Cleo said.

"Humph, wish I could tend to mine. He's never here long enough to get tended to."

"So, he went back on his word about cutting back on work?"

"Yeah," I sighed. "And I miss him."

"I know you do. I'd miss him if he was my husband. He is *something else*."

"Oh, please, Cleo. Scott is the prettiest white man I've ever seen."

Cleo laughed loudly. I loved to hear her laugh. "I think we both did good, Mo," she said.

I heard a knock at the front door and said, "Hey, someone's at the door. I'll call you later."

I opened the door for Wasif and turned back towards the kitchen without a word.

"Still upset with me, I see," he said from behind me.

"Still trying to stir up mess, I see," I replied.

Wasif gripped my arm and stopped me in my tracks. I frowned as I spun around and looked at him. And as suddenly as he grabbed me, he let me go. "I'm…I'm sorry. I don't know why I did that," he said softly. There was a look of urgency in his eyes.

I turned back around and led him into the kitchen where I left him and Sahib alone. I went into the living room and stared at the cartoon on the TV, but I wasn't really paying any attention to it. What the hell was going on with Wasif? He'd never grabbed me like that before. In all the years we were together, he'd never been very aggressive towards me. Part of why I'd liked him is that he'd been so easy-going and accommodating.

Wasif's voice brought me out of my thoughts. "Um, he looks sleepy. Mind if I put him down for his nap?"

I looked up at him, lost for a moment. "Huh? Oh, no, that's fine."

Fifteen minutes later, I met Wasif as he was entering the living room and I was exiting it. "He's asleep," he said, avoiding my eyes.

"Okay."

I walked him to the door just as I did every Monday. I opened it and stood to the side, just as I did every Monday. I waited for him to leave, but he didn't. He stood there with an awkward look on his face. He was staring at me, and it was beginning to weird me out.

"I'm not married anymore," he volunteered out of the blue.

"What?" I asked, my brow deeply furrowed.

"I got a divorce. It was finalized a couple of months ago."

"Oh," I said. What else was I supposed to say?

"I just wanted you to know."

As he turned to leave, I said, "W…why?"

He stopped and looked at me. "Why what?"

"Why'd you get divorced? I thought you two had reconciled."

He looked me in the eye. "Because I finally realized that I could never love her. I could never love her because no matter how tightly I closed my eyes or how hard I wished, she could never be you."

I stared at him for a moment then said, "I'm…I'm sorry."

He shook his head. "No, you're not. You're trying to be nice, but it doesn't suit you, Mo."

I threw up my hands. "Well, damn. Do you just get off on insulting me, Wasif? Fine, then. If you want me to be a witch, I'll be a witch. I don't give a damn about your marital status and you can get the hell out of my house."

He moved closer to me. "I didn't mean it like that. It's just that with you, I always knew where I stood. I knew you inside and out. I knew your personality, and I loved you for who you were."

I stood there and tried to absorb what he was saying to me.

"Wasif, I…" I said and my voice trailed off because I really didn't know how to reply to him.

He gently placed his hand on my cheek and brought his face close to mine. "That's what I've always loved about you. No matter what was going on in my life, you were the same. You were always the girl in the student union. The girl who would stop at nothing to get what she wanted. The girl who always got her way. I loved her so much. I *still* love her."

Before I could utter a single word, Wasif's mouth was covering mine and even after three years apart, his touch felt familiar. He kissed me for a long while. He gently pushed me against the wall and pinned me there as he kissed me some more. He ran his fingers through my hair as he moaned against my lips. There was nothing right about kissing another man in the foyer of the home I shared with my husband with my son asleep only a few feet away. I know that. It was wrong, *very wrong*. But it felt wonderful. So wonderful that I wrapped my arms around him and fully returned his kiss.

And when he began to undress me, I didn't resist. I closed my eyes as we slid to the floor. I laid there and felt his kisses and listened as he whispered the things I longed to hear, *needed* to hear. I listened as he told me how much he missed me and how much he needed me. How he'd never stopped loving me.

"I've been waiting for this day for so long. I've been aching for you, Mo," he said. And when he ran out of words to say in English, he spoke Punjabi. And though I didn't understand all of the words, I felt the love behind them.

He kissed and caressed and loved me like his life depended on it. Right there behind my front door, I let him take me back to a place that was once so familiar to me—to the very essence of his passion. I'd forgotten how it felt to be in his arms and to feel his touch. To smell his scent. To feel the urgency of his need for me. I'd forgotten how Wasif could make me feel. Being with him wasn't better than being with Corey. It was just…different, *very* different. And I enjoyed every second of it.

Chapter 9

"No One To Blame"

God, *forgive me.*

I lay on my bedroom floor in tears, my face buried in the carpet as I breathed the words over and over again.

God, forgive me. Please forgive me for what I have done.

I rolled over and clutched my stomach as I stared at the ceiling and cried. *What have I done?* I wondered. *What the hell is wrong with me?*

I tried to forget what happened earlier that day. I really did. After Wasif left, I tried to go about my daily routine. I tried to cook dinner, but my hands trembled. I tried to clean my house, but my legs felt weak. I tried to watch a movie with Sahib, but I couldn't concentrate. My every thought was of Wasif and what we'd done.

I felt his hands on me, smelled his scent and the very thought of my betrayal was sickening to me. I felt like the dirtiest, most underhanded woman on earth. I had even taken two showers, hoping to wash away my sin. But nothing I tried could erase the fact that I had slept with Wasif in the home I shared with the kindest, gentlest, and finest man on the planet. A man I loved without a doubt. *What is wrong with me?*

I nearly jumped out of my skin when I heard the phone ring. I crawled to the night table and picked it up. "Hello?" I said timidly.

"Hey, baby!" Corey said cheerily. The joy in his voice nearly sent me into hysterical tears.

I choked back an avalanche of tears. "Hey."

"You alright? You sound strange."

"I'm fine. I was cutting some onions and now I'm tearing up a little, but I'm fine," I lied effortlessly. *I really am evil*, I thought.

"Oh, okay. Well, I was calling to let you know we're having company for dinner tonight."

"Company? What company?" I asked as I pulled myself to my feet.

"The coach from Alabama Christian University wants to have dinner with us and offer the boys a scholarship."

"Really? What makes him so special? Tons of schools have offered them scholarships and we haven't had them over for dinner." It was going to be hard enough for me to act like a normal human being around Corey and the boys and he wanted to bring a stranger home?

"Well, he seems nice and the boys like him. Plus, he was really adamant about meeting the entire family—you and Sahib included."

I sighed heavily into the phone.

"Is something wrong, Mona-Lisa? I didn't expect you to be this upset about it."

I shut my eyes tightly and told myself it was no one's fault but my own that I was in a bad mood. This was about the boys' future. I would just have to suck it up and handle things like a woman.

"No. No, it's fine. The more the merrier. See you when you get home."

"You sure?"

"Positive."

"Okay, love you, baby."

"I love you, too."

After we hung up, I went into the kitchen and cried and tried to figure out what I could cook that included onions, *lots* of onions.

***

Coach T, as he asked to be called, arrived right on time for dinner. He was tall with smooth dark brown skin and neatly cut salt-and-pepper hair. He was wearing stiffly starched jeans and a white t-shirt. He was a lean and fit older man with a booming voice.

He firmly shook my hand as he entered the house and said, "Great to meet you, Mrs. Sanders. I've been looking forward to it." His eyes met mine for a brief moment and then he quickly looked away and began talking to Corey. If I didn't know any better, I would've thought this old man was checking me out.

I quietly retreated to the kitchen where I finished up with dinner and began placing the food on the table. I nearly dropped the container of squash casserole when I heard Corey's voice behind me.

"Hey, you need some help?" he asked.

In response, my hand instantly began to tremble. *Get yourself together,* I scolded myself silently. I quickly set the dish down. "Um, sure," I said as my eyes darted from the table to the stove, purposely avoiding Corey.

I tensed when he placed his hand on my arm to stop me. "Hey, what's wrong?" he asked softly.

I shrugged, my eyes glued to his shoes. I just couldn't look him in the face. "I don't know. Just tired, I guess."

He lifted my chin with his hand, forcing me to look at him. "You're eyes are swollen. How many onions did you cut?"

"Too many to count. There's onions in the casserole, the salad, and the soup. I guess I overdid it."

"Well, I know it'll be delicious. Look, why don't you just sit down and let me handle things in here."

I smiled. "Thanks."

Dinner calmed me a bit. The food was good, if I do say so myself, and other than the odd looks Coach T kept giving me, he was a very warm and friendly man and he seemed excited about the boys. I could tell that Morgan liked him but Blair seemed a little indifferent. Coach T and Corey did most of the talking, thank goodness. So my silence didn't seem odd to anyone.

After dinner, Corey and the boys walked Coach T out and ended up having another conversation with him in the driveway. I was in the middle of clearing the table when my phone rang. It was Wasif.

I grabbed the phone and hurried to the living room window to find the guys still engaged in a lively conversation outside. I closed my eyes and tried to catch my breath as I accepted the call.

"Hello?" I said softly.

"Hey," Wasif said, sounding just as uncertain as I felt. "You okay?"

"No," I answered.

"I'm sorry to hear that."

"How…how do you feel?" I asked.

"I feel alive again."

I held the phone, unsure what to say.

"Mo, can I tell you something?"

"If you make it quick."

"Okay. Mo, I love you."

I peeped out the window. "I know that."

"And I need you."

I sighed. "I can't leave Corey. I won't hurt him again, Wasif."

"I'm not asking you to leave him."

I leaned forward and cradled my head in my hand. This was all just too much for me. "Then what are you asking? I need to get off of this phone," I hissed.

"One day a week. Just give me one day, Mo," he said.

"Wasif—"

"Just think about it. I'll let you go now. Love you." He hung up before I could reply. I sat on the sofa and clutched my phone and realized that with one really bad decision, I'd gotten myself in a huge mess.

Chapter 10

"Just Because"

A week had passed and I knew Wasif would be by to see Sahib. I'd been avoiding his calls. Corey was still working like madman, trying to prove a moot point, so I didn't have to put forth any effort to avoid him. The twins were busy with their lives, so they didn't have time to think about what was going on in mine, and Sahib was happy as long as he was taken care of.

That afternoon, when Wasif knocked at the front door and walked past me without even speaking to me, I was actually relieved. He was mad at me, so surely he wouldn't expect me to discuss his ridiculous request. I followed him into the living room where he found a sleeping Sahib. He sat and stared at Sahib intently, never even acknowledging my presence. After a few minutes of silence, I left and went into the kitchen where I started washing the breakfast dishes.

When I felt Wasif's hand on my back, I didn't turn around, because part of me—a part I was growing to despise—wanted him to touch me. He leaned in close to my ear and whispered my name. I closed my eyes and took a deep breath. I turned around to face him.

"Wasif…" I began, but he cut me off by covering my mouth with his. His kiss was deep and passionate and he held me so tightly, I could barely breathe. For a moment, I wanted to give in to him. But thankfully my good sense kicked in and I ended the kiss and backed away from him. He tried to kiss me but this time I had the presence of mind to resist him.

"Wasif, I can't," I said.

He searched my eyes. "Why?"

"Because I love him. I can't do this again, especially not here."

He pushed my hair from my neck and kissed it softly. "I have an apartment here in town now."

"Wasif, I really can't."

"Please, Mo. *Please*," he said—his voice full of more desperation than I'd ever heard from a grown man.

I dropped my eyes and shook my head. "No, I can't."

He cupped my face in his hands and forced me to look him in the eye. "Just one more time. Just once more. Please, babe. I love you so much." He kissed me and before I realized what I was doing, I said, "Okay."

He kissed me again and with such desire; I had to catch my breath before I could follow him to the front door.

Before leaving, he turned and smiled at me and said, "I love you more than anything, Mo. I really do. I'll call you."

And I was left holding the door and my breath until he left.

That evening, I lay in bed next to Corey staring at him as he flipped through a copy of *Muscle and Fitness* magazine. I stared at his handsome face, his powerful arms, and his strong hands. Corey was undeniably attractive, but it was his heart that was the most attractive to me. It was his unconditional love for me that I loved most about him. I knew he deserved my love and fidelity in return. I knew what I'd done with Wasif was beyond wrong.

He flipped to another page and my mind flipped back to Wasif. What was it about him that suddenly made him so desirable to me again? We'd always shared an attraction. As a matter of fact, that was really all we shared and it was essentially the basis of our entire relationship. What I had with Corey ran much deeper than that, so why was I so willing to risk my marriage for a moment of passion with Wasif? It just didn't make any sense at all.

As Corey closed the magazine and turned the lamp off, the thought kept running through my mind: *Why did I do it? And why did I agree to do it again?*

Corey fluffed his pillow and pulled the covers over him as he turned his back to me. "Goodnight, baby," he said with a yawn.

I reached over and softly slid my hand over the muscles of his back. "Baby?" I purred.

"Hmmm?" he replied.

I scooted over to him and wrapped my arm around his waist. "Baby, turn over."

"Mm, not tonight, baby. I had a hard day. Maybe in the morning, okay?"

I laid there and stared at his back in disbelief. Not tonight? Maybe in the morning? Was he serious? It had been weeks, *literally*, weeks.

As I turned over and snatched the covers over my body, I fully realized why Wasif suddenly seemed so desirable to me. At least he wanted me.

***

The next morning, Corey was already in the shower when I climbed out of bed. My head had cleared overnight. There was no way I could make what I did with Wasif Corey's fault. Corey was a good man. The bad person in the equation was me. As bad as I wanted to, I couldn't even blame Wasif for what happened. He did it because he loved me, and I believed that to be the truth. I'd always known he loved me. When he took another woman as his wife, I still knew. The morning he married her, he came to see me first and made love to me, crying and apologizing the whole time. He'd felt that it was out of his control, that he *had* to marry her.

I honestly didn't care all that much about him marrying her. I was only concerned about being taken care of, and he'd promised to do that. When he left her, right before we broke up, it was only because he was afraid of losing me. Because he had to have me. He'd once told me that having me was the only way he was able to stay married. I was the glue that held his life together. And now, three years after our break-up, he'd proven his own words true. He'd divorced her.

As I stood in front of the dresser mirror and inspected myself, I could see his hands on my body; feel his kisses on my neck. His words rang in my ears, *"I feel alive again."*

I shuddered as a chill ran through my body. *Why am I standing here reminiscing about my infidelity with Wasif? Why was I relishing in it?* Then it hit me like a ton of bricks. I remembered how empty I'd felt when Wasif had missed his visit with Sahib that day. My mind reeled as a thought occurred to me.

I'm still in love with Wasif.

Chapter 11

"Body And Soul"

I was at work, quietly re-shelving some returned books and trying to hold on to what was left of my sanity when my cell phone began to buzz in my pocket. I only kept it on in case the daycare or the school called. But the call was from neither place. When I checked the caller ID and saw Wasif's number, I felt an odd combination of excitement and anxiety. I ducked into the ladies room to answer his call.

"Hello?" I said, gripping the phone tightly as I leaned against the cold, tiled wall.

"Hey," he said softly. "You feeling any better?"

I closed my eyes and pressed my forehead against the wall. "I don't know how I feel."

"I love you, Mo," he said. "You'll never know how much."

I sighed and slid until I was sitting on the floor. "Wasif—"

"Meet me for lunch," he said, interrupting me.

"I can't." I knew if I saw him again there was just no telling what I'd do.

"Please."

That one word shouldn't have moved me. It shouldn't have affected me at all. After all, I'm a mother. I'd heard the word more times than I could count. I was supposed to be immune to it. But something about the *way* he said it, the tone and timbre of his voice, made me feel the word like I never had before. Here was this handsome, well-to-do man literally begging for my time. Add all of that up plus the fact that somewhere in my heart I still held a place for him, and all I could say was, "Okay."

I quickly jotted down his address and spent the remainder of the morning trying not to feel like I was betraying Corey. Of course I *was* betraying him, but I didn't want to think about it. I *couldn't* think about it because thinking about it would make me fall apart. I was an expert at holding myself together in the worst possible situations. That's something that my sister and I shared and something that we cherished. We knew what could happen if we fell apart.

By noon, I was so hungry that I no longer felt guilty about lunch with Wasif. At that point I would've been willing to break bread with the boogey man to quiet the rumbling in my stomach. It only took about ten minutes to get to the gated community where Wasif's condo was located. At least I didn't have to worry about being spotted at his house. Neither Corey nor I knew anyone who could afford to live there. When I knocked on his door, I could already smell the food and it smelled heavenly. Wasif came to the door in a crisp white t-shirt and a pair of scrub bottoms. The scent of his cologne mingled with the smell of the food—an odd combination, but something about it appealed to me. He smiled a relieved smile.

"I thought maybe you were gonna stand me up," he said as he led me into the dining room. He pulled a chair out for me. "Wait here. I'll be right back."

As I waited for him, I took in my surroundings. His place was beautiful in an understated way—muted colors and comfortable furniture neatly filled the spaces. I couldn't help but wonder if any of this stuff was from the home he'd shared with his wife. Was I sitting at her dining room table, eating from her dishes?

As if reading my mind, Wasif said, "I hired someone to decorate the place. Everything's new from this table to the silverware. What do you think? Do you like it?"

I nodded. "It's very nice. Why'd you decide to leave Little Rock and move here?"

"So that I can be near my sons…and you." He handed me an absolutely beautiful bouquet of yellow roses.

I took them and looked up at him. "Wasif, you know I can't accept these."

He nodded. "I know you can't take them home with you. But you can enjoy them while you're here. Beautiful flowers for the most beautiful woman in the world."

I cleared my throat and I felt my cheeks begin to heat up. "What's on the menu for lunch? I'm starving and whatever it is, it smells great."

He began to uncover the foil pans that sat in the middle of the table to reveal lobster, grilled steaks, spinach salad, and baked potatoes.

With wide eyes I said, "Oh, yum!"

We ate in silence because I was too hungry and the food was too good to disrespect it by talking. Afterwards, we settled in his cream-colored living room with cups of coffee and talked about the boys and his new practice.

"I'm glad things are going so well for you. I know it was hard to separate from your father," I said.

He tilted his head to the side. "No, he actually made it very easy for me."

I frowned. "What do you mean?"

Wasif sighed and leaned forward, resting his elbows on his knees. "We had an argument. The same one we always had. He told me how stupid I was. How I never should've gotten involved with you. How you were my downfall. He told me I could've had it all, that I threw my future away for a black woman and her illegitimate kids."

"H…he said all of that?" I knew he wasn't my biggest fan, but that was just harsh.

He nodded. "Yeah."

"What did you say?"

"I told him that I loved my sons, and that I loved you." He reached for my hand and I let him grasp it. "Mo, that day I finally realized something."

"What?"

He looked deeply into my eyes. "That I don't need his approval to be happy. Plus, he won't give it to me, anyway. The only thing that will make me happy is you."

I dropped my eyes. "Your children make you happy."

"They do, but I can't be completely happy without you, Mo." He leaned in and kissed me softly. "The last three years I have felt so empty, so alone…" his voice trailed off and a single tear rolled down his cheek. My eyes were glued to him as he continued to speak. "You are the only woman I've ever loved."

"You…you never loved your wife at all?"

He sighed. "I cared about her. She's a good person and she should've been a good wife, but my heart was already taken. It's always belonged to you, Mo—*only you*. On our wedding night, I sat in my car for hours while she waited for me in the hotel room. I sat in the car and stared at you and the boys' pictures. I cried until I finally fell asleep. She called my father and told him I was missing. When he found me on the parking lot, he was so angry with me.

"He told me to be a man and to do the right thing. He's my father and I've always feared and respected him. So I tried, I really tried to do the right thing, but now I realize that the right thing would've been to marry you." More tears fell and he wiped his face with hand. "I'm sorry for not being man enough to stand up to him and do the right thing by you."

"It…it's okay, Wasif. I understand."

"No, it's not. But if you'll let me, I'll make it up to you."

"Wasif, I'm married to Corey. I don't understand what you want from me. I don't know what I can give you."

"I want *you*; however I can have you…whenever I can have you. And when the time comes, I know I will have all of you."

"Wasif…I don't know."

"Okay, look me in the eye and tell me that you don't love me anymore. Tell me you didn't want me the other day and that you didn't enjoy it."

I dropped my eyes.

"Say it and I'll accept it and I'll leave you alone."

I looked into his brown eyes that were so full of pain and love. "I can't say that. Not truthfully."

He leaned in and this time, he planted a long kiss on my lips. "Tell me you love me," he whispered.

"I do," I said softly.

He reached for my hand and pulled me to my feet. It felt like we floated through the living room to his beautiful bedroom...to his huge bed. One by one, he plucked the petals from the roses until the bed was a blanket of fragrant yellow. And he was right; I really did enjoy those roses.

***

I ended up spending the entire afternoon in Wasif's bed. I called off sick at work and left Wasif's in time to pick Sahib up from daycare then rushed home to make a quick dinner. As I pulled into my driveway, my stomach was in knots of guilt, but at least there was no one home. Maybe I'd have time to pull myself together. I could still smell Wasif's cologne on me although I'd showered before leaving his place. A second shower was definitely in order.

I unlocked the door, and Sahib rushed into the living room and turned on the TV. I headed to my bedroom and nearly jumped out of my skin when I saw Corey sitting on the side of the bed. I was so startled that I dropped my purse.

His eyes were fixed on me as he said, "Where've you been? I've been trying to reach you."

I bent over to pick up my purse. "Where's your car?" I asked. "I didn't see it in the driveway."

"I had a wreck during lunch. That's why I've been trying to reach you."

"A wreck!" I rushed to him, inspecting him for injury. I found none. "Are you okay?"

"Yeah, I'm fine, but my truck's totaled. Some idiot ran right into the passenger's side. Why haven't you been answering your phone?"

"Well, I, uh, I went shopping and I left my phone in the car."

"Your boss said you left for lunch and took the rest of the afternoon off because you weren't feeling well."

"Yeah, I kinda lied to her. I just didn't feel like being there."

"You should quit. We don't need the money anymore," he said proudly.

"Yeah, I'll think about it. You sure you're okay?"

"I'm fine."

I stood from the bed and headed to the bathroom. I was in the middle of undressing when Corey said. "What'd you get?"

"Huh?" I said.

"You said you went shopping. What did you get?"

"Oh, nothing. I just window-shopped really. Didn't see anything I liked."

I was naked and had just turned the shower on when I felt Corey hug me from behind. "I see something I like," he whispered in my ear.

Really? Today? Right now? I groaned inwardly. Truthfully, Wasif had worn me out. I wasn't sure if I had it in me to be intimate with Corey. I thought for a second and said, "Sahib's in the living room. If we're in here too long he'll get into something."

"I'll make it quick," he said.

I shook my head. "You know how I feel about quick. No, sir."

He backed away. "Fine, fine. Turn me down," he said playfully. He left the bathroom but I wouldn't get off so easily at bedtime.

Chapter 12

"Perfect Love Affair"

It was my mother's fault. She was the reason I was so messed up. She was a mean, evil, selfish woman who loved men more than her own children. I loved my children more than any man, but I had the mean, evil, and selfish thing on lock. Selfishness was the reason for the affair. I wanted both of them. I loved both of them for different reasons. But I didn't love either of them enough to let the other go.

Now that I think about it, I'd never really let Wasif go at all. Even when I married Corey, I still held onto him in my heart without even realizing it. He was a part of me, father of two of my sons, and maybe that bond was much stronger than I'd realized. There was a passion between us that was undeniable.

At the same time, I loved Corey from the depths of my heart. He was good to me and good *for* me. He loved and respected me. There was nothing he wouldn't do for me. He was the one person in the world whom I was sure would lay down his life for me.

Somewhere in my jacked-up heart, there was room for both of them. In my mind, I needed both of them. And in my flesh, I desired both of them. That's the way it was, and as time went on, I grew to be comfortable with it. I gave Wasif his one day a week, sometimes two. But I was still Corey's wife, and I always would be. It was the best of two very different worlds for me.

I sat on the side of Wasif's bed and stared out of his huge bedroom window as he planted kisses on my bare back. He ran his hand through my hair and I closed my eyes and smiled.

"Come back to bed," he whispered.

"You know I can't. You know I've gotta go."

"Yeah, I know. Come here for a second."

I laid back and let him kiss me. I could tell he was about to start something up that I didn't have time to finish. I gently pushed him away. "I've got to go."

I quickly showered and redressed and as I headed out the door, gave him another kiss. Imagine my surprise when I saw Corey knocking at the door next to Wasif's. He didn't see me because he had his head down, looking at his phone. I ducked back into Wasif's place and quickly shut the door behind me, my heart thundering in my chest. A second later, I realized Corey wasn't just looking at his phone, he was dialing my number.

Wasif gave me a questioning look, and I shushed him as I

answered Corey's call.

"Hello?" I said, clutching my forehead and trying to sound as normal as possible.

"Baby? Hey, what're you up to?"

"Nothing. Just getting ready to pick Sahib up. Um, what are you up to?"

"Oh, uh, just grading some papers. Probably gonna be late coming home. Just wanted to let you know."

I felt my chest tightening. He was lying to me. Why was he lying? "Oh, okay. See you later then."

I hung up and slumped onto Wasif's sofa with my jaw dropped.

"What's going on?" Wasif asked.

I looked up at him. "Who lives next door to you?"

"A nurse. I work with her from time to time. Why? What happened?"

The tear fell before I could stop it. "I…I think Corey's cheating on me."

Wasif sat beside me and held me as I cried like a baby. Did I have a right to be upset? Of course not. But I was. I was the bad person in our relationship—*not Corey*. I was supposed to make the mistakes. I always hurt him, not the other way around. How could I have been so blind, believing that he was a man of his word? I'd been so preoccupied with my own affair, I didn't even notice his. The possibility of Corey being unfaithful never even occurred to me.

I had to wait for two hours for Corey to leave before I could leave. I had Blair pick up Sahib and some pizzas for dinner. Wasif kept check of the parking lot so that he could let me know when Corey left. I was thankful that I always had sense enough to park far from Wasif's building. I was sure that Corey hadn't seen my car. But why did I care anyway? He had parked his rented truck right in front of the building for all to see.

The worst part of the situation was the wondering. Wondering what was going on next door. Was he touching her the way he touched me? Was *she* touching *him*? Was he in her bed? Was she whispering his name like I did? Did he love her? My thoughts were deafening inside my head and Wasif's walls were thick, thank God. The waiting and wondering nearly drove me out of my mind. If I'd actually been able to hear them, I surely would have lost it.

I was finally able to leave and when I made it home, I went straight to my bedroom to find Corey in the shower. I angrily slipped out of shoes and sat on the bed, waiting for him. When he finally emerged from the bathroom, I had to catch my breath. All of that personal training seemed to have defined the muscles that rippled through his body. I hadn't noticed how much more toned he'd become until that moment. For a second I forgot what I was even mad about. Then he smiled and bent over and kissed me. *Oh, yeah. He's cheating on me.*

"Hey, baby. Where've you been? I was getting worried," he said.

"Oh, just out and about. It's amazing the people you can run into around here," I said, eying him.

"Oh, yeah? Who'd you see?" he asked as he began to towel off.

"Oh, just someone from high school. She's going through a tough time. Her husband's cheating on her," I said, watching him closely.

"Oh, man. Really? Who is she? Do I know her?"

"I doubt it. Anyway, she's really upset."

"I bet. I'm sure she's devastated."

"I know I would be."

He dropped his towel, walked over to me, leaned over, and planted a long kiss on my lips. "You'll never have to worry about that happening. I'm all yours and only yours."

Boy, he's an even better liar than I am. I forced a smile. "Good to know."

"Well, did you talk to her? You should've invited her to church tonight."

"I tried to talk to her, but she has her own plans for handling the situation."

He pulled on his underwear and then a pair of gym shorts as he looked up at me. "Oh yeah?"

"Yeah, she said she's gonna get even. You know, have an affair, too."

"Wow, I hope you told her that's not the answer. Two wrongs never make a right."

I stared at him for a moment. Could he really be this good at deception? If so, could I believe anything he said? "I know, but I can understand why she'd feel that way."

"It's still wrong. " Corey pulled a t-shirt over his head and then looked at me for a long moment. "That conversation must have really gotten to you. You look upset."

I wanted to yell at him that I'd seen him at that woman's door. I wanted him to know that I knew. I wanted to tell him about my month-long affair with Wasif. I wanted him to hurt like I was hurting. But the only words that came out of my mouth were, "I'm okay."

He reached for my hand and said. "Good, let's go eat."

I followed him from our room to the kitchen without another word. What a pair we were.

Chapter 13

"Baby"

My period was so late that I had just about accepted the fact that I was pregnant by someone. Didn't have a clue who the father was. When my period finally came, I nearly shouted with joy. The last thing I needed to add to this whole sordid mess was another child. I promptly started another pack of pills, glad to have dodged a bullet.

I was silently thanking God when I answered my sister's phone call. "Hey, long time no hear," I said.

"The phone rings both ways, you know?" she said with a smile in her voice.

"Yeah, I'm sorry about that. Things have been quite interesting around here."

"Oh, do tell. Besides one of the horses giving birth, it's been boredom city around here, but I'm not complaining. We've had enough drama and trauma around here to last a lifetime."

I told her about my suspicions about Corey, leaving out my own infidelity. But I didn't fool her.

"How'd you happen to be in the same apartment building as Corey?" she asked.

I held the phone, trying to formulate a decent lie.

"Oh, no, Mo. Does Wasif live there?"

I sighed. "Yes."

"Mo, you're not—oh, you are, aren't you? How long?"

All of a sudden, I felt a deep sense of shame. "A month or so."

"Mo…"

"But that doesn't make what Corey's doing right."

"Mo, you don't know *what* Corey's doing. You don't know that he's cheating. You just jumped to a conclusion."

"Why else would he lie to me?"

"I don't know, but I don't think he's cheating on you. Look, I know all about irrational. I almost lost my family being irrational and jumping to wrong conclusions and doing stupid stuff. You need to pray about this, Mo. And you need to talk to Corey, But most of all, you need to leave Wasif alone."

I was silent.

"I know this is not what you want to hear, but it's the truth. I love you, but I can't go along with you when you're in the wrong."

"I've gotta go, Cleo," I said curtly.

It was her turn to sigh. "Okay, call me later, when you're not mad at me."

I ended the call and tried to block her words out, but I couldn't. When was the last time I prayed about anything? We never missed church, but I hadn't paid attention to a sermon in weeks. I'd just been going through the motions. I closed my eyes and prayed for the truth to be revealed to me. I hoped that when it was, I would be able to handle it.

***

I was on my way home from Wasif's when Corey called. His voice was full of excitement. "Hey, where are you, beautiful?"

"On my way home."

"Well, hurry. I have a surprise for you."

I took my time picking up Sahib and driving home. I was sure whatever Corey had to tell me was of no interest to me. When we made it home, Corey was sitting in the living room with a bouquet of roses in one hand and a piece of paper in the other. He was grinning from ear to ear. He rushed to me and Sahib and handed me the flowers before picking Sahib up and spinning him around.

"Hey, little man," he said, kissing Sahib's cheek. Sahib giggled and when Corey set him back on the floor, he ran to the TV and turned it on. That boy loved him some cartoons.

"Hey, baby," he said brightly as he kissed me on the cheek.

"Hey, what's going on?" I asked.

He handed me the paper and waited anxiously as I read it. "This is a deed?" I asked.

"Yes. I bought some land just outside of town, and I'm having us a house built."

I was speechless.

In his excitement, he didn't seem to notice my shock. "I bought the land from this nurse I met at the gym. It belonged to her parents and she sold it to me at a good price."

"A...a nurse?" I said, feeling a little light-headed.

"Yeah, it was so hard keeping this a secret from you. I even had to meet her at her place a couple of times. I was scared to death someone would see me and think I was having an affair or something. But it was worth the trouble to see the look on your face right now," he said with a light chuckle.

"Uh, uh, yeah," I said with a fake chuckle of my own. I looked down at the paper. "Wow, I can't believe you did this."

"Yeah, and look," he said as he pointed to the paper. "Your name is on it, too."

"I don't know what to say."

He smiled. "Surprised?"

"*Very.*"

"Well, I have more news."

"I think I should sit down." I sat on the sofa and Corey sat down beside me.

"We need to pick out a floor plan for the house. I want construction to start this summer."

"Okay."

"And I've put in my resignation at the school. Next year I'll be a full-time personal trainer. No more late nights coming home. My evenings and weekends will be reserved for my family again."

I looked into his eyes and saw how proud he was of himself. At that moment, I shared in that pride. My husband was an incredible man. A man I'd been taking for granted. I vowed to never do that again.

I placed my hand on his cheek and said, "I'm so proud of you, baby."

"Thank you. That's all I've ever wanted to do—make you proud to be my wife."

"I've always been proud to be your wife and I always will."

"I love you, Mona."

"I love you, too, Corey."

Chapter 14

"Do You Believe Me"

For two weeks, I managed to dodge Wasif by making up excuses and just not answering his calls. Evidently, two weeks was his limit. He showed up at my doorstep on a Wednesday with a concerned look on his face. I let him in, knowing I was going to have to end things with him. I wasn't looking forward to the conversation.

He visited with Sahib for a few minutes and then followed me into the kitchen. "Mo, what's going on?"

My eyes were glued to the floor as I said, "I can't see you anymore, Wasif. I'm sorry."

"Why?"

"Because it's not right."

"Nothing is more right than us being together."

"I love Corey. I can't keep doing this to him."

"What he doesn't know won't hurt him."

I looked up at him. "It's over, Wasif."

He stepped closer to me, his eyes pleading with mine. "Please don't do this." He fell to his knees and wrapped his arms tightly around my waist. "I'm begging you not to do this. *I love you, Mo.*"

I looked down at him and shook my head. "Wasif…"

He buried his face in my blouse and his voice was muffled as he spoke. "Please, just give me a chance. Give me a chance to give you what you deserve."

I closed my eyes and rested my hand on his head. "What do you mean? What do I deserve?"

He looked up at me as he tightened his grip on my waist. "My devotion…and my name. A real house, a new car—whatever you want. You deserve all that and more. You deserve more than Sanders could ever give you. You deserve to be treated like a queen and I want to do that for you. If you let me, I'll do anything you want. Just, please, babe. *Please.*"

How many times in the past had I wished for him to say those words—hundreds? Thousands? But it was too late now. Much too late.

I pried myself from his grip. "I love Corey. This is over. It *has* to be over. I'm sorry, Wasif, but this is just how things have to be," I said firmly.

Wasif stood to his feet. "Mo, I'm trying to make things right with you. I'm offering you my heart and all you've got to say is you're sorry?"

"Yes, *I'm sorry*. I really am. I care about you, but I can't—no—I *won't* break Corey's heart again! He didn't deserve it the first time and he doesn't deserve it now. This—is—over!"

He closed his eyes. "Okay, you don't have to leave him or anything like that. At least not right now. Just…just don't say it's over. Just let me be with you."

I turned my back to him. "No."

"I'll take Sahib."

I spun around and faced him. "What?"

"I'll take him. I will take him to Pakistan."

I studied his face. He looked serious, determined even. "You don't even like Pakistan," I challenged.

His eyes narrowed. "I'll learn to like it."

"I don't believe you."

"Fine. Don't believe me. But if you are not at my place at lunch tomorrow, watch what happens."

He left and I felt my stomach drop. Would he actually take my baby from me?

I didn't have long to mull over the situation. No sooner than I heard the door swing shut behind Wasif, the phone rang. I walked into the den and answered it without checking the caller ID.

"Hello?" I said as I sat on the sofa and tried to rub away the dull headache that was beginning to form.

"Mrs. Sanders? Coach T, here."

Lord, I don't have time for this right now. "Um, hi, Coach T. My husband and sons are at school right now."

"Yes, ma'am. I figured as much. I'd actually like to talk to you."

I closed my eyes and laid my head against the back of the sofa. "Um, I don't wanna sound rude, but this is just not a good time. Can you call another day?"

"Well, yeah, I guess so. Um, well, goodbye."

"Goodbye."

I hung up and sat still, soaking in the peaceful quiet of my house. It only took a minute for me to realize that it was *too* quiet. I opened my eyes and looked around the living room—no Sahib. His toys were scattered on the floor, and the TV was still on, playing Spongebob at a low volume. I hopped to my feet and hurried through the house, He was nowhere to be found. I checked in the backyard, the front yard, the garage. He was gone.

Then it hit me. *Wasif.*

My hand trembled as I dialed the number. I didn't give him time to say "hello." As soon as the call connected, I screamed into the phone, "Do you have Sahib?!"

Wasif answered with an even "Yes."

For a second, I felt relief, but it was almost instantly replaced with panic. "Why did you just take him without telling me?"

"To show you just how easy it would be. If I wanted, I could drive right to the airport, board a plane and you'd never see him again."

My head began to throb. "Wasif, please bring him home."

"Do you understand now that I'm serious?" he asked.

My breathing became erratic. I felt like I was suffocating. "Please bring my baby home, Wasif," I pleaded.

"Say it and I will."

"Say what? What do you want me to say?!"

"Tell me it's not over between us."

"Wasif, please just bring him back."

"*Say it*, Mo," he demanded.

Tears began to fall faster that they'd ever fallen before. "It's not over between us."

"Be at my place tomorrow at noon."

I held the phone as I continued to sob.

"Mo, did you hear me?"

"Yes. I heard you. I'll be there. Please bring my baby back."

"I'm pulling into the driveway now."

I hurried out the door, to Wasif's SUV, and snatched the passenger door open. I grabbed Sahib and quickly walked back to the house.

"See you tomorrow, Mo," Wasif called from behind me in a sadistically cheery voice.

I stopped in my tracks and sat Sahib down in front of the door. "Stay right here, okay? Mama will be right back."

He nodded and I quickly walked back to Wasif's car. As he began to back out of the driveway, I pounded my fist on the hood of his vehicle. He screeched to a stop and rolled his window down.

"What the hell—" he began, but I quickly cut him off.

"*You love me?* Really, Wasif? Is this what love is to you? Threatening me with my child, *our* child? I can't believe I felt bad for you. Bad enough to start sleeping with you again!"

He frowned. "Oh, so that was the only reason, Mo? Because as far as I could tell, you were enjoying our time together as much as I was."

"You are a sick, sadistic man. I don't know how I could've ever loved you!"

He shook his head. "You want this as much as I do. You just don't wanna hurt Sanders. I'm merely helping you do what you're too afraid to do. We belong together and in the end, we *will* be together."

He backed out of the driveway and after five minutes of standing there staring at the empty spot where his SUV once sat, I walked back into the house and held Sahib closely for as long as he let me.

Chapter 15

"Squeeze Me"

I gave Wasif what he wanted, whenever he wanted it, wherever he wanted it—his place, my place when Corey was at work, the library when I was at work. I had trapped myself in a mess. Had I never started up with him again, things would never have gone this far. I was convinced of that. I'd unwittingly opened up a trap door and now I was freefalling. Things were totally out of my control and that was a position I hated. It reminded me too much of my life growing up, of my mother and the things she subjected me and my sister to.

As a child, I'd rightfully felt powerless. But now, as an adult, it just felt wrong and I didn't know how much longer I could go on. Would Wasif really expect me to keep doing this indefinitely? He hadn't said anything about me leaving Corey, but I had a feeling that that was inevitable. I was sure he was working towards making that demand, but what would I do then? Despite my stupidity, I loved Corey and I never wanted to leave him.

I lay in bed with Corey's heavy arm across my waist crying as I did every night of recent. Crying and praying that God would show me what to do to free myself of this situation. I bit my lip as a sob threatened to break free. I wiped my silent tears and sucked in a deep breath, trying to calm myself.

"What's wrong, baby?" Corey asked. His voice was clear, as if he'd been awake for a while.

I cleared my throat and tried to sound normal, but I failed. My voice broke ever so slightly as I spoke. "Nothing. I'm fine."

He moved his arm and effortlessly rolled me over to face him. "You're my wife. You think I don't know when something's wrong with you? That's why I woke up. I could sense it. Why are you crying?"

I couldn't answer him. All I could do was cry harder. I buried my face in his bare chest and cried and moaned and groaned. He rubbed his hands up and down my back and kissed my forehead and assured me that everything would be alright because he was there and he would always take care of me. And with every word from his mouth and every touch of his hands, I felt worse and I cried harder. At that moment, I knew I was going to lose him. Maybe not right that second, but eventually I would. Because if I had to choose between losing my baby or losing Corey, I would choose losing Corey. Any mother could understand that. Logically, I understood it, but my heart was breaking nonetheless. For the first time, I realized that what I'd felt for Wasif wasn't love—not really. We shared passion and lust and maybe even a little fondness, but the thought of losing him never felt as agonizing as what I was feeling. What I had with

Corey was real, true love. And I knew that once I lost him, I'd never be the same again.

As my sobs began to quiet, Corey said, "You wanna talk about it?"

I shook my head.

"Did you dream about your mother?"

I took the cue, thankful for a way around telling him the truth, and I slowly nodded.

He kissed my forehead. "Tell me, baby."

I searched my mind for a memory. Something that could account for my tears. It didn't take long for me to find one.

"It was my mother's birthday. I was nine and Cleo was five…"

She wanted to go out and celebrate, but she couldn't find anyone to keep us. So she took us with her to the club. She laid some blankets out in the backseat of her boyfriend's old car and told us to lie down and go to sleep. It was the middle of the summer, so she left the windows cracked so we could breath. Cleo managed to fall asleep, but I couldn't. The music was loud—I could hear it every time the doors to the club swung open, which seemed like ever half a second. I sat and watched drunken people mill in and out of the club. I saw a man pee next to the front door. I saw a woman on her knees in front of a man. I had no idea what she was doing down there, but the man seemed to enjoy it.

People walked by laughing and shouting at each other and then a couple of guys, one older and one younger, came. They were arguing loudly. There was a woman standing between them, trying to keep them apart. They argued for a good while and people started to drift out of the club to watch them. I'll never forget how the older guy's voice sounded when he said the words.

"Y'all want each other? You can be together in hell!" he said. Then he shot the younger guy in the head. By the time the second shot came, I'd ducked under the covers with Cleo. I could hear people running and screaming and crying. There were more shots and more screams and I was so scared. One of the bullets hit one of the windows in the car. By that time, Cleo had awakened and she was crying. So was I.

We laid there in the back seat for so long, I thought we'd have to spend the rest of our lives back there hiding from the man with the gun. From underneath the covers, I could hear the police and ambulance sirens. I hugged Cleo tightly and kept the covers over our heads. Even as we began to sweat, I didn't move. I was just too scared.

When Mama and her boyfriend finally made it back to the car. I heard him fussing about having to get his window fixed because of the bullet hole. The car had been moving for a few minutes before Mama lifted the blanket and looked at us. "Good," she said. "Y'all didn't get y'all selves shot or nothing. That's the last thing I need right now."

"Later on, I heard Mama say that man shot and killed three people along with his girlfriend and her lover," I said into Corey's chest.

Corey rubbed my arm soothingly. "I'm so glad you weren't hurt. If something had happened to you, I would've never gotten the chance to love you," he said into my ear.

His words brought me back to the present, back to my betrayal and the pain in my heart. The tears returned. "Corey…" I croaked.

"You're safe with me, baby. I'll never let anything happen to you."

"I love you so much, Corey."

He kissed my forehead. "I love you, too, Mona-Lisa. And I always will."

Chapter 16

"No One In The World"

Coach T was over for dinner again, touting the benefits of the boys attending his college and playing for his team. I only half-listened to him. I was physically and mentally exhausted from the Olympic-style sexcapades that Wasif was subjecting me to. I never thought in a million years I would ever say I was tired of having sex, but I was. It took me all these years to realize that Wasif actually equated sex with love. It was all he thought about. It was all he wanted from me. We never talked or spent time just being with each other. It was just sex, sex, and more sex. *Is this what it would be like to be his wife?* I wondered.

I looked over at Corey who talked to me and held me and loved me. We shared passion and our sex life was great when he wasn't too tired, but it was never just about the sex with him. It was so much more, and I was throwing it away. But what choice did I have? I couldn't let Wasif take my baby from me.

I closed my eyes and chased all thoughts of Wasif or losing Sahib or losing Corey from my mind. I focused on the conversation in time to hear Coach T say, "So, Mrs. Sanders, where did these boys get all of this natural talent?"

I smiled. "I have no idea. I guess somewhere on my side of the family." I could've said that Morgan inherited his talent from Corey, but that didn't explain where Blair's talent came from since Wasif was his father.

"I see. Well, they have bright futures ahead of them, and I want to be a part of those futures."

I nodded. "I can see that, but really, the final decision is up to them. What you do you think, boys?" I asked, looking from Blair to Morgan.

Blair smiled. "Well, I like what I hear. I'm thinking seriously about choosing your school, Coach T. If what you say about their pre-med program is true, it would be a perfect fit for me."

I smiled proudly. Blair had always wanted to follow in Wasif's footsteps, and with his brains, I had no doubt that he would. "What about you, Morgan?" I asked, noticing that Morgan had been uncharacteristically quiet throughout dinner.

He cleared his throat and looked from Coach T, to Corey, to me. "Well, I guess this is as good a time as any. Um, I've decided not to go to college right now."

"What?!" I said—shocked. I'd always told both of them how important college was. I'd been drilling that into them since they were little boys.

"Then what do you plan on doing, Morgan?" Corey asked calmly.

"I wanna travel and see the world. I've been saving up the allowance my other dad gives me, and I've been looking for a job for after school. I mean, we all know that I don't have Blair's brains. I'm not some big scholar."

"So you're never going to college?" I asked. "You're just going to aimlessly drift around the world?"

He sighed. "No, Ma. See, I knew you'd take it the wrong way. I'll go eventually—when I'm ready. Right now, the last thing I wanna do is be up in some classroom all the time."

"What about basketball? I thought you loved to play," Corey interjected.

"I do and if these were pro scouts instead of college scouts trying to recruit me, I'd jump on it. College just ain't for me right now."

I looked at my son and wondered what in the world was going on in my life. I was throwing my marriage away, and Morgan was throwing his life away. It was just all too much for me. I stood from the table and said, "Please excuse me."

I left for my room and sat on the side of the bed trying to process Morgan's revelation. He'd been sent to one of the best private schools in the state and had received an excellent education and it was all for nothing? I was deep in thought when I felt Corey sit down on the bed next to me.

"Where's our dinner guest?" I asked.

"Gone. You upset?" he asked.

"Yep. Aren't you?"

"Actually, I think we should hear him out. After all, it's his life, Mona. Whatever decision he makes, he'll be the one who has to live with it."

"I know that, but I can't just sit by and watch him throw his life away."

"I'm not trying to throw my life away," Morgan said from the doorway. "I'm just trying to live my life the way I wanna live it."

"No, you're being irresponsible. You're not thinking about anything or anyone but yourself. You're throwing away all I've done to ensure you have a good future," I said angrily.

"How is this about you, Mama? It's my life!"

"It's about me because of the sacrifices I made to be sure you had the best of everything. You've been trying to throw your life away for months. First the drugs, now this nonsense. No! You are *not* doing this!"

Corey placed his hand on my arm. "Mona—"

I snatched away from him. "No, Corey, he's gonna listen to me."

Morgan slumped his shoulders; a look of defeat clouded his face. He shook his head as he turned to leave.

"Mona, you need to hear the boy out. It's *his* life," Corey said.

I turned my head and glared at him. "First of all, you have no right to oppose me when it comes to him. *You* didn't raise him, I did!" As soon as I flung the words at him, I wished I could take them back.

Corey's eyes flashed with a combination of hurt and anger as he walked across the room, grabbed his keys, and left.

I trotted in behind him, following him all the way through the house out to the driveway. "Corey, I'm sorry. I didn't mean that."

He unlocked his truck and climbed inside without a word. He didn't even look at me when he slammed the door shut. I was left standing in the driveway watching him back away with tears in my eyes.

Corey didn't come back home that night. As I stood at the stove cooking breakfast, I felt like what was left of my world had fallen apart. He wouldn't answer his phone and he didn't even call to check on us. He left me. Corey left me.

"Mama, the bacon is burning," Blair said, snapping me out of my thoughts.

I looked down at the pan of sizzling, charred bacon and began to cry as I switched the stove to off. I grabbed a dry dish towel and wiped my face.

Sahib hopped up from the table and trotted over to me. He hugged my legs and said, "It's okay, Mama."

Blair walked over to me and pulled me into a hug. "It's alright," he said softly.

"I'm sorry," I whispered.

"What's going on?" Morgan said as he entered the kitchen.

I shook my head. "Nothing for you all to worry about."

"Where's Coach?" Morgan asked.

That did it. I burst into tears again. All three boys were hugging and comforting me when Corey walked into the kitchen. We all stood there looking at him and him looking at us as if none of us knew what to do or say. It was Sahib who made the first move. He ran from me to Corey and jumped into his arms. "See Mama, he's home," he said cheerily. What a smart little boy.

At that moment, I forgot about any pride I had left. I dropped it right there in that kitchen. I walked as fast as my legs would carry me to Corey and I collapsed in his arms. "I'm so sorry, Corey. I'm so sorry."

He wrapped his free arm around me and said, "I know. It's okay." And for that brief moment, I believed him. Everything was okay.

Chapter 17

"Caught Up In The Rapture"

"Is something wrong?" Wasif asked.

I was sitting on the side of his bed staring at the view outside the window. "I'm tired," I said. Drained was more like it. As much as I loved Sahib, I just didn't think I could carry on with this affair.

"Of me?" he asked.

I turned and glanced at him then stood and began to redress. "I can't do this today, Wasif. I just can't."

"Can't do what? I think we already did it," he said with a smile.

I sighed. "Reassure you or pet you up or whatever it is you want me to do. My marriage is falling apart, but that's what you want isn't it?"

He sat up on the side of the bed. "I just want you, Mo."

"Yeah, I know," I said mournfully.

"What do *you* want?"

I pulled on my shoes. "I'd tell you if I thought you really cared."

He reached over and gently rubbed my arm. "I do care."

"Yeah, right," I scoffed.

He stood from the bed then reached down and cupped my face in his hands. "I really do, Mo."

I looked him in the eye and saw again the boy I'd once loved so much. "I want for this to be over. I want a normal life with my husband without fear of losing my baby boy."

"I can't give you that, Mo.

"There's nothing else I want from you."

"I'm sorry. I love you too much to let you go."

I stood and pulled the strap of my purse over my shoulder. "I just don't understand how you could think threatening to take my child from me and basically blackmailing me into sleeping with you translates into love."

He frowned a little as he stood in front of me, still naked. "Can't you see? I'm doing all of this *because* I love you. I'll do anything to keep you in my life, Mo. *Anything.*"

I shook my head and sighed as I turned to leave.

"One day you'll understand and it'll all make sense to you," he called after me.

"No, I don't think so, Wasif," I said as I turned the door knob and left.

***

A couple of weeks later, I woke up with a start, trying to figure out where I was. The room was dark and unfamiliar and the arm that was draped across my waist was too light to be Corey's. Then it hit me. I'd fallen asleep in Wasif's bed. I threw his arm off of me and stumbled to my feet, still disoriented. Was it early evening or late at night? Just how long had I been asleep? Was Corey looking for me?

My eyes darted around in the darkness, trying to locate my clothes. I could feel tears forming in my eyes. *I messed up. I really messed up this time.*

A lamp popped on and I heard Wasif's groggy voice. "What's going on?"

I glared at him. "It's dark outside. I should've been home by now! What time is it?"

Wasif reached over to the bedside table and picked up his watch. "10 PM," he said as if it was normal for a married woman to be out that late.

A deep sense of panic hit me. "Oh my God, *Sahib*! Oh, Lord, I left him at the daycare."

Wasif stood from the bed and walked over to me. He rested his hand on my shoulder and I promptly snatched away. "Blair picked him up," he said.

"Blair? What? How?" I asked as I frantically pulled my shirt over my head. There was no time to shower. I needed to get home as soon as I could.

"Well, he texted you to see if you needed him to pick up anything before he made it home. At first, I thought it was my phone until I saw the message. I saw how soundly you were sleeping and you're always talking about how tired you are, so I didn't want to disturb you. I texted him back and told him to pick Sahib up so you could keep napping."

I stared at him incredulously. "You answered my text? Did anyone call me?" *Did Corey call me?*

He nodded. "Well, Sanders did."

I held my breath and felt my heart begin to race. I look of shear dread shadowed my face.

"I didn't answer it."

I released the breath and slipped my feet into my shoes.

"He called a bunch of times so I finally just shut your phone off," he said as he bent over and pulled his underwear on.

"What?!" I said.

"Well, like I said, I didn't want to disturb you while you were sleeping and that ringing phone was eventually gonna wake you up."

I shook my head as I walked towards him and stuck my finger in his face. "No, you are just trying to ruin my life by purposely sabotaging my freakin' marriage! You turned my phone off? How in the hell am I supposed to explain this?!"

He shrugged. "Why don't you just stay here until the morning? That way you'll be rested and your mind will be clear enough to talk to him."

"You are crazy as hell if you think I'm spending another second here!"

I stormed out of the condo and stomped all the way to my car. How could Wasif be so damned conniving? Blackmailing me for sex wasn't enough for him anymore. Now he was trying to force me into leaving my husband or my husband into leaving me. I prayed all the way home. I didn't want to lose Corey. God in heaven knew that was the truth.

After I parked in my driveway, I sat in my car and stared at my house. I was so afraid to go inside, afraid that this would be the last time I entered it as Mrs. Corey Sanders. I took a deep breath and prayed for the umpteenth time before finally leaving my car and slowly entering my home.

I walked softly into my bedroom. Corey was already in bed, sleeping quietly. I was hoping to ease into bed and avoid having to explain where I'd been until the morning. I was headed to the bathroom to undress when I heard the lamp click on. *Damn!*

I turned around to see Corey sitting on the side of the bed staring at me, "Where've you been, Mona-Lisa?" he asked softly.

I just stood there, mute. I had no clue what to say to him.

"Or should I ask you who you were with?"

I remained silent, staring at Corey as if it was the last time I'd see him.

Corey stood and walked over to me. He leaned over until his face nearly touched mine. "I can smell him," he said. "I can smell his cologne." His brow creased into a frown. "Is that a passion mark?!"

I quickly turned around and looked at my reflection in the mirror that hung on the bathroom door. Sure enough, there—as plain as day—was a passion mark on my neck. *Damn, damn, damn!*

I turned and looked at Corey then almost instantly dropped my eyes. "Corey, I…"

"You were with *him*. I know you were." He placed his hands gently on my arms. "How long have you been seeing him, Mona?"

I felt the tears as they began to trail down my cheeks. "About three months. I'm so sorry."

He backed away from me with a stricken look on his face. "Three months?" He backed into the bed and sat down.

I nodded as I began to wring my hands. "I didn't mean for it to go on like that."

He looked up at me for a moment then he reached for the lamp and threw it against the wall. I jumped. "You cheated on me with *him*?!" he said, raising his voice. "I love you and you promised you were done with him. You promised!" He stood from the bed, walked over to the wall, and leaned his forehead against it.

I slid to the floor and buried my face in my knees. "I'm so sorry…*I'm so sorry*…"

"Why, Mona? Why can't you just love me back? That's all I need you to do."

I looked up at him. He was now standing over me with a pained expression on his face. "I do love you, Corey. I…I was lonely. You were always gone and you didn't have time for me. And you know I just don't like being alone," I said weakly.

"I was trying to take care of you and the reward I get is you cheating on me? You're ungrateful as hell!"

"Corey, wait, let me finish."

Corey walked over to the dresser and raked everything to the floor. "Finish?! Let you— "

"Hey, father or not, if you touch my mama, it's gon' be me and you." I looked up and saw that it was Morgan who spoke. He was standing just inside the doorway. Blair stood behind him holding Sahib's hand. Blair looked ready for action, too.

I shook my head. "Boys, go back to bed," I said, my voice trembling.

Corey walked over to Morgan who now matched him in height. They were nose to nose as Corey spoke. "I'd never lay a hand on your mother. You should know that. I'd tear the walls off of this place before I hurt her. "

They stood and stared at each other for several minutes before Morgan finally backed down and he and Blair left with Sahib. Corey closed the door behind them and walked back to the bed where he laid on his face. I crawled to the bed and climbed in with him. I laid my head on his back and wrapped my arm around his waist. "I tried to stop seeing him, but he threatened to take Sahib and leave the country. Corey, please, *please* forgive me," I whimpered.

Corey just lay there, as still as a stone. He didn't say a word. He was so still that for a moment, I wondered if he was breathing. But then he finally rolled over and I sat up. He sat on the side of the bed, his back facing me.

"Corey. Corey, please forgive me. I love you so much."

He turned, and I could see that his face was wet. "You don't hurt the people you love, Mona," he said softly. "As a matter of fact, you do everything you can *not* to hurt them."

"I know and—"

"But *you*...you've hurt me over and over again."

"Corey—"

"How can you love me when you obviously don't know what love is?"

"I know now. I know now that I love you with all my heart."

"You know *now*? Now that I'm leaving you?"

His words punctured my heart, and I could barely breathe. "No...no...no, please don't. Please, Corey. I'm begging you not to go."

He shook his head as he stood from the bed and walked over to the closet. Panic overtook me when I saw him pull a duffel bag out and begin to haphazardly stuff it with his clothes.

I rushed to him and grabbed the bag, slinging it across the room. "You can't go, you can't leave me," I said, desperation in my eyes and my voice.

"Yeah, I can," he said, stone-faced. He moved toward the bag but I beat him to it. I took it and held it behind me.

"Mona, give it to me."

"No, I don't want you to go."

"You shoulda thought about that before you spread your legs for your damn baby daddy."

Tears continued to fall. "I was wrong, and I'm sorry, Corey. I'll never do anything like this again. Please forgive me."

"You were with him *here*, weren't you? You were with him in our home, in our bed. I thought I smelled his cologne in here the other week, but I told myself I was imagining things. I was right, wasn't I? It *was* his cologne and you slept with him in *our* bed, didn't you?"

I looked up at this beautiful man, my heart literally breaking, and said, "Yes, because he made me."

"He *made* you?" Corey jeered.

"Yes, he made me. He threatened to take Sahib from me. He threatened to take him out of the county if I—"

"Answer one question for me, Mona."

"O…okay…"

"Did you ever cheat on him?"

With a furrowed brow I said, "What? Who?"

Corey moved closer to me, his eyes filled with hurt and rage. *"Who?* Who else, Mona? You know who the hell I'm talking about!"

I closed my eyes. "Corey—"

"No!" he shouted. "Tell me. All those years the two of you were playing house and raising *my* son—*my only child*, did you ever cheat on him?"

"No," I said softly.

"No," he scoffed. "It's obvious who you really love, isn't it? He gets your undying loyalty, he gets to raise my son, he—" he stopped speaking as his voice began to break.

I reached towards his face, but he backed out of my reach. "Corey, you're who I want. Please, believe me. I love *you*."

He chuckled softly than gripped the back of his head and groaned loudly. "No-you-don't!" he shouted.

I grabbed his hand. "Yes, I do!"

"You don't even understand what the hell love is!"

"I do understand. *You* are love, Corey. *You are.*"

He yanked his hand from my grip and stared at me for a long, painful moment. "Yeah, well *love* is getting ready to walk out the damn door. I tell you what, keep the bag. I'd rather walk out of here naked before I spend another night with you." He left the bedroom barefoot and dressed in pajama bottoms and a t-shirt, and seconds later, I heard the front door slam. I dropped the duffel bag on the floor and began to pace the room. I didn't know what to do with myself. When my cellphone rang, I rushed to it, instinctively knowing it was Corey.

"Hello? Baby?" I said anxiously. My heart was beating a mile a minute.

"Yeah, you know what I said about not laying a hand on you?"

"Y...yes."

"Well, that doesn't apply to Dr. Feelgood. You might wanna know that I'm on my way to beat the brakes off of him. I know where he lives."

Click—he hung up.

I dropped the phone and stared at it. Part of me wanted to call and warn Wasif, but a greater part of me wanted him to get hurt. So instead of calling Wasif, I tearfully cleaned up the mess Corey had made of the room and placed the duffel bag back in the closet. And then, exhausted from everything that had occurred, I curled up in my bed and fell asleep.

Sleep didn't last long. Around two in the morning, there was a knock at my front door. I bolted upright in bed, excitement filling me at the thought of Corey standing on the other side of the door with open arms, but then reality set in. I knew better than that. Corey wouldn't be that forgiving or at least not that quickly. I'd betrayed him, in our own bed, no less. No, it couldn't be Corey at the door. Besides, he had a key. I'd made it to my doorway when Morgan passed by me on his way to the front door.

I inched down the hall behind him with Blair behind me. Morgan looked through the peep hole and his eyes were wide as he glanced at me then opened the front door. On the other side of the door stood Wasif sporting two black eyes and a busted lip.

Chapter 18

"How Could You"

My hand flew to my mouth as Wasif stumbled into the house clutching his side.

"Dad, you okay?" Morgan asked as he helped him walk into the living room.

Wasif eased down on the couch and winced. "Yeah, I need to talk to your mother. Alone."

Morgan and Blair looked at both of us and then left the living room. I stood in the doorway and stared at Wasif. Corey had beaten more than the brakes off of him.

Wasif was breathing heavily as he looked up at me and said, "Why didn't you let me know you were gonna tell him about us? I could've used a warning."

"Because I *never* intended to tell him. He figured it out when I came tipping home late, thanks to you."

"Yeah, well, I guess I paid for it. I think he broke a rib."

"A rib? With his fist?"

"No. He kicked me after I fell, which was after he punched me about ten times. Oh, and did I mention that he spit on me after he kicked me?"

I shook my head. "Wow, I would say that I'm sorry…."

"Don't waste a lie on me. You're probably glad he beat me up."

"And you're probably gonna press charges against him."

"But you don't want me to, do you?"

"Of course not. But you're gonna do it anyway. Anything to make my life more miserable than it already is."

"No—I'm just glad he's out of the picture. Now, we can be together."

I stood and stared at him. Was he serious? Did he think I could just move from Corey to him so simply? Before I could tell him he was out of his mind, the front door flew open. And Corey marched into the living room looking like a mad man.

"Did I not make myself clear earlier, Kwaleeb?!" he bellowed as he charged towards Wasif.

Wasif looked up at him and nearly whispered, "It's *Wasif*."

"Oh, really? You think you got the right to correct me, *Waheed*?

In my own house?! On my damn sofa?!"

Wasif dropped his eyes. "Look, I was just saying—"

"You were just saying? Maybe I should *just* finish kicking your ass."

I watched as Corey drew his fist back. I grabbed his huge arm. "Wait, Corey, don't," I said.

He looked down at my hand on his arm and then glared at me. "I know the hell you are not defending him. I *know* you're not!"

I vigorously shook my head. "No! I'm looking out for you. I don't want you to get in any trouble. That's all."

Wasif looked at me. "I will never understand why you left me to marry this racist."

"I ain't no damn racist. I don't hate all Pakistanis, I just hate *you*!" Corey screamed.

"Yeah, well, the feeling is mutual!" Wasif yelled.

"Look, would you two stop this?! The boys are right down the hall," I interjected.

Corey closed his eyes and released a frustrated sigh. "What the hell are you here for?" he asked Wasif through clenched teeth. "Do you *want* me to kill you?"

Wasif leaned forward and buried his face in his hands. "I...I love her."

"She is my wife. *My wife.* You don't get to love her. You don't have the right to love her!"

Wasif shook his head. "She was mine first."

Corey clenched his fists. "Only after you *took* her from me and even then she wasn't yours. She was *never* yours. You two weren't married. She was just your damn sidepiece. She was *not* yours!"

Sidepiece? What the hell? "Hey!" I said with a frown.

Corey turned his attention to me. "What were you then, Mona? Huh?"

I dropped my eyes.

"*Exactly,*" Corey said. "I made you my wife, Mona. My *wife!*"

By then, Morgan and Blair had returned to the living room and were staring at Corey. He shifted his gaze from me to Wasif to the twins. Then he shook his head and said, "I tell you what, I'll leave this little happy family alone." He headed towards the door but stopped in his tracks when he heard a small voice say "Coach?"

Corey turned around to see Sahib standing in the hallway rubbing his sleepy eyes. He walked over to Sahib and squatted down in front of him. "What ya doing up so late, little man?" he asked.

"I had a bad dream. Can I sleep with you and Mama?"

Corey looked from Sahib to me as if he was trying to figure out how to answer him. He smiled at Sahib and tousled his thick hair with his hand. "Well, how about I tuck you back into your bed and help you chase the bad dream away?" he finally said.

Sahib smiled and then wrapped his arms around Corey's neck. Corey lifted him from the floor and carried him back to his bedroom. My heart felt like it was splintering in my chest. Corey was such a good man and I had ruined everything. I was suffering and so was Corey, but most of all, my sons were suffering from my careless, foolish actions. I swallowed a huge lump that had formed in my throat and suddenly began to heave. I clutched my stomach and looked over at Wasif, whose eyes were trained on me. "You…you need to leave," I told him.

"Me leave? I'm injured and you want *me* to leave? I need some help, here," he said, giving me an incredulous look.

I closed my eyes as my stomach continued to lurch. "This is Corey's house. Please leave, Wasif. Just leave."

"Mo, I'm hurt!"

I sighed heavily. "Well, you're the damn doctor! What the hell can I do?!"

Wasif jumped a little at the tone of my voice. "I…" His voice trailed off as I'm sure he was trying to think of another excuse to hang around.

"Dad, I can drive you home if you need me to," Blair said softly. I hated that the boys had to witness this mess, but what could I do?

Before Wasif could answer Blair, Corey returned to the living room. He walked over to Wasif, stood in front of him, and said, "I'ma say this one more damn time. If you lay another finger on my wife, it's gonna take Bin Laden's ghost and all of the active members of Al Qaeda to peel me off of you!" With that, he turned and looked from me to the boys. I looked over at the twins who wore confused and concerned looks on their faces. I'm sure their expressions mirrored my own.

Corey looked back at Wasif and added, "I'll get out of y'all's way now. I know I'm not welcome here. Hell, I never was."

As he stalked towards the front door, I trotted behind him and grabbed his arm. "Wait!" I pleaded. "Please stay and talk to me."

Corey stopped but didn't turn to look at me. "Let me go, Mona."

I kept my grip on his arm. "Please, baby, don't go."

"Mona-Lisa, the man you've been cheating on me with is sitting in my living room right now and it's taking all of the Jesus within me not to go back in there and beat his brains out. If I stay here, it is going to take some serious divine intervention for me not to kill him. I need to leave and I need to leave *right now*."

I let my hand fall from his arm to my side. "O…okay. Will you call me tomorrow? S…so we can talk?"

"Mona, I don't even know where I'm sleeping tonight, let alone what I'll be doing tomorrow."

"You can sleep here."

"*Mona…*"

"Okay, okay. I…I love you, Corey," I said.

He stood there for a moment and I think instinctively he almost reciprocated, but he didn't. "I'm sure you do," he said sarcastically.

"I really do."

"Yeah," he grunted. He gripped the doorknob, but before he could open the door, I said, "Wait! What…what if Sahib wakes up looking for you again?"

With his hand still on the doorknob, he turned and looked at me. His expression was cold—not angry, not sad, but cold. "I am not his father," he said. "I only have one child, remember? And let's face it, I'm not his father, either. So, I tell you what, you and Dr. Strangelove can have it—*all of it*. I'm sure y'all can handle things. He can pay your bills and raise your sons and treat you the way that suits you best…like a whore." With that, he left, taking with him the very foundation of my heart.

I stood there staring at the closed door, unsure as to what to do with myself. His words had hit me like several tons of bricks and yet, I wasn't angry at him. I just…missed him. I missed him and loved him and needed him. And he was gone.

He was gone.

I let my eyes fall from the door to the floor. I kept them glued to the floor as I slowly walked from the foyer, past my sons and my lover, to my bedroom where I climbed into bed and pulled the covers over my head. I lay there and stared into the darkness and wished this was all a horrible dream. But I knew wishing was a colossal waste of time.

I heard the footsteps of someone entering my bedroom. I closed my eyes and wished them away, but no such luck. The next thing I heard was Wasif's voice.

"Mo?" he said softly.

"Go home, Wasif," I said from underneath the covers.

"Well, I was wondering if I could spend the night here. My ribs are so sore; I don't think I can take the ride home."

I snatched the covers from my head and stared at him. Was he serious? "What?" I asked.

"Can I stay here?"

"No, this is Corey's house. *You need to go.*"

"Mo, come on."

I reached over to the night table, grabbed my phone, and threw it at him, missing him by a mile. "I said no! *Hell*, no! GO HOME!" I shrieked.

Wasif turned and hobbled out of my room. I pulled the covers over my head and after offering a weak, ineloquent prayer to God, I fell into a troubled sleep.

***

The next day was Saturday. I spent that day in bed, only getting up to use the toilet. I didn't shower and I couldn't eat. Blair and Morgan took care of Sahib because I couldn't do that either. Corey didn't call and Wasif wouldn't stop calling, and all I wanted to do was disappear.

Sunday brought more of the same. No Corey, too much Wasif, and unending pain for me. I missed church that morning, but I was determined to make the evening service. Though I have to admit, I wanted to be there more for the chance to see and talk to Corey than for the sermon or the fellowship.

I walked into the sanctuary, took a seat on my regular row, and searched the sparse crowd for my husband. I'd just about given up hope of him showing up when I saw him slip in through one of the side doors My heart skipped a couple of beats as I watched my big, fine husband take a seat near the front. I wanted to move closer to him. I wanted to sit right next to him and hold his hand like I usually did during service. I wanted him to wrap his arm around my shoulder and smile down at me. I wanted to be with him so badly.

But I didn't move a muscle. I just sat there, my eyes glued to him. The boys didn't move either—having decided their allegiance was with me. Sahib was in the nursery; otherwise, he would've definitely left me for Corey.

I stared at him, my heart aching like never before. I half-listened to the choir. And I can't even recall what the message was about. The only thing on my mind was that I missed my husband. Even sitting in the same room with him, I missed him so much. Sunday night, I climbed into bed still wearing my church clothes and searched for sleep that I never found. Around midnight, I got out of bed and began to pace the floor. I paced the entire house and cried until the sun rose.

Monday morning, I pulled myself together enough to get Sahib ready for daycare and fix the boys breakfast. But as soon as the door closed behind them, I retreated to my bed where sleep continued to evade me.

It was around noon a week later when I heard a key turn in the front door. My heart leapt. I was sure it was Corey, and though I knew I looked a mess, I didn't care. I raced to the door to meet him.

He was closing the door behind him and when he turned and looked at me, I thought I would die. He looked so sad and disheveled. I'd hurt him badly—that was plain to see.

"I just came to get some of my stuff. Please don't try to stop me," he said softly and then brushed past me.

I followed him into our bedroom and sat on the side of the bed. I watched as he began to pack the same duffel bag we'd scuffled over. I wanted to stop him, but I also wanted to just stare at him, to commit his face and his body to my memory. I loved him so much.

As he bent over to pick up a pair of shoes from the closet floor, I walked over to him and hugged him from behind. His body stiffened for a second and then he relaxed. I laid my head on his back and closed my eyes. "I'm so sorry," I whispered. "I miss you. *I love you.*"

Corey let his hand rest over mine for a moment before prying my arms from his waist and turning to face me. "Is that supposed to be enough? You apologizing and saying that you love me?"

I looked into his eyes. "I *know* it's not enough, but it's all I have to offer right now. I love you, Corey, and I need you. Please come back home." I reached up and kissed him softly on the lips.

He closed his eyes and shook his head. "You don't love me, Mona-Lisa. You didn't back in college and you don't now."

I lifted his t-shirt and kissed his chest. "I do love you. I love you so much."

He rested his hand on my back. "You couldn't love me and do the things you did."

I returned to his lips and kissed him deeply and I felt him return the kiss. "But I do. Let me show you how much."

He didn't resist. He let me show him my love on the bedroom floor, in the bed, and in the shower. He even called off from work for the rest of the afternoon and stayed right there with me. He left just before the boys made it home from school with a promise to call me later that evening.

Chapter 19

"You're My Everything-Revisited"

Corey didn't call me that evening. As a matter of fact, he didn't call me the rest of that week. When he finally did call me, he sounded distant and strained.

"Hey," he said.

"Hey, baby," I said as I sat up in the bed. As strained as his voice sounded, it was still wonderful to hear from him.

He cleared his throat. "How are you and the boys?"

"The boys are fine but Sahib's been asking about you. I've been missing you. I was waiting for your call."

"Um, I needed a little time to think."

I pulled the covers off of my legs and sat up on the side of the bed. "About us?"

"Yeah. Look, Mona-Lisa, I'm just gonna be straight with you. I…I want a divorce."

I gripped the phone tightly. "What?" I'd heard him wrong. Either that or I was losing my mind. He couldn't have said the word *divorce*.

"I want a divorce," he repeated.

I stood from the bed and began to pace the floor. "How…what do you mean? We were just together the other day. That didn't feel like you wanted a divorce!"

He sighed into the phone. "That…that was a mistake. I didn't mean to mislead you. I love you, Mona, and I can't just turn that off. But I can't be with you anymore—not if I can't trust you."

"Please, Corey, please don't do this! What happened to for better or for worse? What happened to that?!"

"Mona, this is way beyond worse. I…I can't be with you anymore. Just…just expect to hear from my lawyer."

I held the phone, swallowing tears and searching the walls of my bedroom for nothing in particular. I had never in all my life felt a pain like the one I felt at that moment. Not even labor pains compared in severity. *Is this how Corey felt when we were in college? When I left him for Wasif?*

"Mona, are you still there?"

"Yes." My answer came out as a pained croak.

"I'll keep paying the mortgage for now, so don't worry about that.

If you need anything, you can always call me."

I need YOU. "Where are you staying?" I asked through tears that fell in rapid succession.

"I got my old apartment back. Luckily, it was vacant again."

Luckily. "O…okay," I said.

"Well, I'll talk to you later, Mona." Then he hung up.

"I love you," I said to the dead phone line. Then I threw my phone across the room and watched it crash into the wall and fall to the floor in pieces. I stared at it for a few minutes then I stripped the bed, tossing sheets and pillow cases all over the room and screaming at the top of my lungs at the same time. I walked to the closet and snatched my clothes off of the hangers, ripped them up, and threw them from one side of the room to the other. I raked jewelry and change from the dresser, smashed perfume bottles against the wall, dumped make-up into the toilet, and ripped the shower curtain from its rings. I screamed and yelled and cried and destroyed things until I was drenched in sweat, and then I fell to the floor. All the while, my little dog howled and barked. I guess I was upsetting her, or probably scaring her.

Hours later, I heard my sons enter the house. I kept my eyes closed as I lay amongst the shredded clothes and broken perfume glass. My arms and thighs were cut and bleeding. My wounds stung from the perfume that covered them but I didn't mind the pain. As a matter of fact, I welcomed it because for a brief moment, it took my mind off of the piercing ache in my heart. I whimpered and sniffled as Lizzie sat on the floor beside me and whimpered, too. I hated for my children to see me like that, but I was too hurt and too weak from heartache to move. If I'd had my way, I would've disappeared—vanished into thin air. To not exist would have been much better than the agony I was feeling.

I heard heavy footsteps and then Blair's voice. "Mama!" he said, sounding alarmed. "Morg! Mama's hurt! Don't bring Sahib in here."

Next I heard Morgan. "Mama! Oh no. This is my fault. This is all my fault!"

The last thing I heard before I drifted off to sleep was Blair's anxious voice. "We need to call 911!"

***

Everything was so hazy. *Where am I? Who is talking? Why do my eyelids feel so heavy?* I tried to open them but couldn't. I strained my ears, trying to better hear the muffled voices.

"Blair, Morgan, you two can head home. Sahib needs to be in his bed." I was almost sure that was Corey's voice.

"But, Coach—" Morgan began.

"No, Morgan, I agree. You three need to head home. Your mom is fine. Everything's gonna be okay." Was that Wasif?

"O…okay," Morgan said skeptically.

I heard a door close and then I heard Corey's voice again. "Now that they're gone, I can say what's on my mind. You need to get the hell out of here."

"No, I'm here to check on Mo, and that's what I'm going to do." It was definitely Wasif.

"Are you insane?!" Corey asked in a harsh whisper. "What makes you think you have the right to be here at all?"

"Because I love her, and she is the mother of my sons."

"Please don't make me whoop your ass up in this hospital. *Please*."

"Look, I don't want to fight you."

"I know you don't because it wouldn't be a fight. It would be me kicking your ass and you taking it."

"Can I just have a moment alone with her?" Wasif asked, sounding defeated.

"Nope."

"Will you tell her I was here?"

"Nope."

"You can't keep us apart."

"I have a ring and a marriage license that says different. Now get the hell out."

"She'll come back to me. She always does."

I heard the door close and then I felt a hand on my cheek. I continued to struggle to open my eyes to no avail.

"I love you, Mona-Lisa," Corey whispered and then kissed my forehead.

"I love you, too," I screamed in my head and then...silence.

***

The first thing I saw when I awakened from heavy sedation was Wasif's concerned face hovering over me. I eyed my surroundings and quickly realized I was in the hospital. Had I dreamed Corey was there?

I returned my gaze to Wasif. "You came to take Sahib from me?" I whispered.

His expression changed from one of concern to one of surprise.

"No. No, the boys called. I'm here for *you*. Are you okay?"

I reached up and gripped my throbbing head and felt my eyes well up again. "No. Has my husband been here?"

Wasif's expression hardened, but I was hurting too much to care. "Yes" was all he said.

It was real. It wasn't a dream after all. He was here and he said he loved me. "Where is he? I want to see him."

"He spent the night at your bedside. He left this morning."

I sat up and my head began to spin, so I quickly lay back down. I raised my arms and inspected the bandages that almost entirely covered them. "The night? I've been here all night? What time is it?"

"Two in the afternoon."

"Where are the boys?"

"I sent them home. They were here most of the night."

"Sahib, too?"

"Yes."

I closed my eyes. "I need to see Corey."

"He's…he's gone, Mo."

"I need to call him but I broke my phone."

"Mo, why don't you rest yourself for a while?"

"Give me a damn phone, Wasif!"

Without another word, he handed me the bedside handset. My hands trembled as I dialed Corey's number. It rang straight to voicemail, so I left him a message and then laid the phone next to me in the bed. I closed my eyes and prayed that he'd call me back.

Wasif stood there for a moment and then said, "Do you want me to leave?"

"Yes," I said without a second's hesitation.

"Okay. I'll check on you later. I love you, Mo."

I didn't answer him. I just turned my back to him and closed my eyes.

I laid there and waited for Corey's call. An hour or so had passed when I heard a soft knock on the hospital room door. I turned over in time to see Corey walk into the room, worry creasing his brow as he slowly walked towards the bed.

I blinked back tears. *"Corey..."*

He stood by the bed and stroked my cheek with the back of his hand. A single tear rolled down his cheek and landed on my face as he leaned over and kissed my forehead. "What did you do to yourself?" he asked.

I grabbed him and pulled him into a hug before he could back away from me. He leaned into me and I could feel his body shake as he sobbed. We cried together for a while before he finally pried himself loose from my grip.

"I love you, Corey. I'm not gonna make it without you. Can't you see that?"

Corey wiped his face with his hand. "I can see that you're hurting. So am I."

"Then forgive me and come back home."

Corey stared down at me. "It's just not that simple."

"Why not? Don't you still love me? You said you did."

He closed his eyes, ran his hand over his hair, and sighed. "You know I do."

"And I love you. It doesn't get any simpler than that."

Corey shoved his hands into the pockets of his jeans and sighed. "Look, I better go. I don't want to upset you. I'll check on you later."

"Corey—"

He shook his head and placed his hand gently on my cheek. "Later, okay? I promise to call you later."

I nodded and watched him leave the room. I laid there with my mind reeling, trying to figure out how I was going to win my husband back, because I *had* to win him back. I wondered if Corey knew my cell phone was broken. Did I tell him on my message? If not, I needed to tell him. I didn't want to miss his call. So I scrambled out of bed. I didn't have a robe, so I reached around and pulled my hospital gown closed with my hand. I held onto it as I slowly walked across the cold linoleum to the door.

I opened the door and looked right, then left. I saw Corey standing at the nurses' station talking to someone. I called his name, but at the same time, someone dropped a food tray and the commotion that followed drowned out my voice. I was weak and had to move slowly, but I finally made it to him and when I did, I my heart dropped. He was talking to the nurse who lived next door to Wasif.

Chapter 20

"In My Heart"

I can't explain why I did what I did next. Well, that's a lie. I *can* explain it. I was hurt and upset, and well, to be blunt, I was mad as hell that he'd left my room just to walk out there and start up a conversation with *her*. He'd been to her house, for business so he said, but the way she was looking at him told me she had more than business on her mind. *Much more.*

So I walked up to Corey and tapped him on his shoulder. He turned and gave me a shocked look. "Hey, baby," I said. Then I turned to the nurse and said, "Let me introduce myself, I'm his wife." She opened her mouth to reply, but before she could, I flew across the desk and grabbed a handful of her hair, or at least the hair she'd most likely purchased and had glued to her head. She screamed as I straddled her and punched her in the mouth.

I was going in for another punch when I felt someone pull me off of her. I struggled to break free of their grip, kicking and screaming some pretty bad stuff at the nurse the whole time. I think I said some of the Punjabi cuss words that Wasif once taught me, too. I even managed to land one of the kicks against her thigh.

I kicked and screamed with no regard to the fact that the hospital gown was flying open and I had no underwear on. I bucked backwards and head-butted the person who had ahold of me and they let go with a groan. I turned around to see that it was Corey.

He was doubled over, gripping his head. "Mona, what the hell is wrong with you?!" He shouted as he looked up at me through squinted eyes.

"Me?!" I shrieked. "You were such a damn hurry to leave. Is *she* the reason you can't come home?! Huh?! Is she?!"

There was a crowd of hospital workers and patients and passersby surrounding us now, taking in every second of the spectacle.

Corey just stood there and shook his head.

I slapped him. "Is she?! Is she the reason you can't forgive me?"

I moved my hand to slap him again, but he grabbed my arm and stopped me. Then he pulled me towards my room.

"Answer me!" I shouted.

Corey dragged me into my room and slammed the door behind us. I jerked free of his grip. "Are you sleeping with her?!" I demanded.

"No!" he shouted. Startled, I eased backwards until the backs of my thighs touched the cold metal of the bed rails.

He moved towards me and brought his face close to mine. "No, Mona, I have never been unfaithful to you with *anyone*. I have never even *looked* at another woman. I love you. I know you have issues, and I love you anyway. I love your flaws just like I love the good things about you. But that mess you just pulled? You put your damn hands on me?! That made up my mind for me. You are crazy as hell and it is over between us!"

"No, it can't be over *because* you love me."

He shook his head and glared at me. "I wish to God I didn't."

And then he left, slamming the door behind him. I stood there and watched as the door vibrated on its hinges. And then I passed out.

***

I was severely dehydrated as a result of the many days I barely ate or drank when I was home. And according to the psychiatrist they sent in to talk to me, I was also having a nervous breakdown. I guess all of the abuse of my past plus the trauma of losing my husband had caused my little brain to snap. Who knows?

When the psychiatrist, Dr. Montague, came in to talk to me, I just stared at him. I wasn't going to share my secrets or my shame with some stranger in wire-rimmed glasses whose own fingernails looked like he'd been nibbling on them. If he had bad nerves, how the hell was he going to be able to help me with all of my mess? No, he wasn't going to work out at all.

I listened to him drone on about stress management for thirty minutes before I finally told him that I wanted a female therapist but I probably would've taken anyone but him. He looked more relieved than anything. I was sure he was glad to be rid of me and my hysterics. A little later, a social worker came in and asked if there was anyone available to help take care of Sahib other than Blair and Morgan while I was recovering. Recovering? Recovering from what? How does one recover from screwing up his or her own marriage?

I told her that Wasif would be helping out. I didn't bother asking him, because I knew he'd be more than glad to hang around. And so, after a week in the hospital, I was sent home with a prescription for an antidepressant and an appointment to see a female psychiatrist. But even in my jacked-up mental condition, I knew that more than anything, I needed someone to hold my hand and pray for me.

And that's just what God sent me. Blair drove me home and when I opened the door, the house was filled with the scent of something heavenly being whipped up in the kitchen. And in the kitchen was a sight that brought me to grateful tears. There stood my little sister, as beautiful as ever, her unruly hair pulled away from her face with a colorful headband. When she saw me, she stopped what she was doing and rushed to me and pulled me into the most comforting hug anyone has ever given me.

She sat me down at the table and placed a huge plate of lunch in front of me and watched me eat, her eyes full of genuine compassion. In between bites of food, I looked up at her and thought to myself that she was the most beautiful sight I'd seen in a very long time. From her copper skin to her round brown eyes to the huge mass of hair on her head, my sister was breathtaking. But then again, she'd always been the most beautiful woman in my family—even as a child she was lovely. I'd often thought that was why my mother mistreated her—she was jealous of her.

After I finished eating, I smiled at her and said, "Thanks for the food and thanks for coming. I know you have your own life to deal with."

"What else are sisters for?" she asked. "Besides, when Corey called, I couldn't get here fast enough."

I frowned slightly. "Corey called you?" I'd thought that maybe one of the twins called her.

"Yes. He wanted me to know you were in the hospital. He's worried about you."

"I don't believe that," I scoffed. "Seems to me he can't wait to get rid of me. He refuses to give me another chance."

Cleo reached across the table and rested her hand on top of mine. "Mo, he loves you, but he's hurt. You have to put yourself in his shoes. Wasif has always cast a shadow over your marriage. He's always around as a reminder of what he once meant to you. It probably would be easier for him if it was anyone other than Wasif."

I nodded. "I know. I just wish there was some way I could save my marriage, but there's not. It's over and there's nothing I can do about it and knowing that I'm so powerless is driving me crazy." I pulled the prescription and appointment card from my pocket. "See?"

Cleo looked down at the slips of paper and then back up at me. She shook her head. "You're not crazy. You're hurting and being hurt can make us do some crazy things. I know all about that. Therapy can help, Mo. So can the medicine. It will keep you from lying around missing meals and being incapacitated. Remember, no matter how bad you feel, your sons still need you. All of them, not just Sahib."

A single tear began to trickle down my cheek. As I wiped it away, I said, "I don't want to take that medicine and I don't want to go to a therapist."

"Then what do you want to do?" Cleo asked.

"I…I want to get my husband back. No matter what it takes. I want Corey back."

Cleo nodded. "Okay, then the first thing you need to do is work on you. You need to work through some things before you can be a wife to him."

I stood from the table and walked over to the sink. I leaned against it and peered down the drain. "But I don't have time for that! He's probably already filed for divorce. By the time I get myself together, it will be too late!"

Cleo walked over to me and placed her hand on my shoulder. "If it is in God's plan for you two to be together, and I believe that it is, then you can take all the time you need and it won't be too late."

"How do you know that? I mean, I can stall him; I can refuse to sign the papers for a while. I can even contest the divorce, but I can't stall him forever."

"I know because I know that you love each other. Love always makes a way. Where there is love, there is always hope. All you gotta do is try, Mo and keep loving your husband and you've gotta pray for your marriage. Everything will work out."

I nodded. I wanted so desperately to believe her.

Cleo took my hand and pulled me back to the table. "Now, if you don't want to see a psychiatrist, maybe you could try a Christian counselor, or even your pastor. But you need to talk to someone, Mo. I can contact my counselor and see if she knows of anyone you can try here."

I smiled. "I think that would work better for me."

Cleo pulled out her cell phone. "I'll see if she knows anyone who does couples counseling, too."

"But I doubt if Corey will agree to couples counseling."

"He might not agree to it today, but he will eventually. He loves you, Mo. He really does and as bad as you're hurting right now, I don't think it even compares to what he's feeling."

I leaned forward and rested my head on the table. "I hurt him. I always hurt him. I wish I knew why."

"Well, maybe you'll find out in counseling."

"Maybe so."

"And the next order of business is for us to do something about your hair. When was the last time you combed it?"

"Girl, I don't even remember," I said and then for the first time in weeks, I laughed and so did Cleo. "Cleo?"

She placed the phone to her ear and said, "Yeah?"

"Will you pray with me?"

She laid the phone down and grabbed both of my hands. "I sure will. Dear Lord…"

Cleo stayed with me for two weeks and it was the best two weeks of my life.

Chapter 21

"Priceless"

The counselor's name was Brianna Swaggert and when I walked into her office, my first instinct was to take off running back out the door. The idea of sitting down with someone and baring my soul was scary—*really* scary. What if I didn't like what I found out about myself? Okay, who was I kidding? I already didn't like a lot of things about myself. Talking to this woman couldn't make me feel any worse.

I saw Brianna twice a week. And I soon realized why God had paired me with her. She was tough and straight-forward, and she wasn't afraid to get in my face. She was just what I needed.

I poured my soul out to her. I told her about my mother—her abuse. I told her about losing Cleo and the hole it left in my heart and about my friendship with Corey and how it kept me from losing my mind.

"Did you love Corey when you were teenagers?" she asked.

"I did. He was someone I could count on. He was a constant. Before him, I never had a constant," I replied.

"And now, as his wife, do you feel the same way about him? Is he still your constant?"

"He was, until I messed things up."

"Okay, let's talk about that. *The affair.*"

I swallowed hard. I had been dancing around that subject for weeks. "O…okay."

"Why did you have the affair?"

"Why? I don't know," I said with a shrug. "I guess I was lonely and I needed to feel needed. Wasif has always needed me."

"Is that the purpose Wasif serves in your life? He makes you feel needed?"

I shrugged. "I guess. Well, he's always said he can't live without me. He says I'm the best thing in his life."

"And what does Corey say about you?"

"That he loves me, and I'm the most important thing in his life."

"Do you love Wasif?"

"I thought I did for a long time. And I guess in some ways I do. But not the way I love Corey."

"So you love Corey more?"

I nodded. "Much more."

"Why?"

"Because he is so good to me. He's always there to hold me when I'm hurting. He takes care of me. He loves my boys—all of them—like they're his own. He works hard to provide for us. And he's so brave. You know, his parents were against him marrying me, to the point that they even refused to come to our little wedding. He told them he respected their opinions and he understood their concerns, but he was going to marry me anyway. Wasif never did anything like that for me."

"Okay, taking all of that into account, let me repeat my question. Why did you have the affair?"

I closed my eyes and shook my head. "Because I'm a damn fool."

She shook her head. "Come on, Mona. That's not the answer."

I was growing frustrated. "Then I don't know why!"

Brianna scooted to the edge of her seat. "Yes, you do. You're a very intelligent woman. Why did you do it? What is it that you thought Wasif could give you that Corey couldn't?"

I leaned back in my chair and wracked my brain. The same word kept bouncing around inside of my mind. *Why? Why? Why?* I sat there for several minutes. I sat and thought until my head began to hurt. And then I opened my eyes and said. "He feeds my ego. Wasif feeds my ego and he makes me feel powerful. I feel like I can control him—or at least I did until he started threatening to take my baby from me."

Brianna smiled. "And what was the one thing that was missing in all of the other situations in your life—your mother's abuse, your sister leaving you, Corey refusing to let you help him and working all of the time?"

I looked up at her slowly. "Control. I had no control over those situations and that made me feel powerless."

"And that, Mrs. Sanders, is the whole thing in a nutshell."

That was my breakthrough moment. That was the moment that everything began to make sense. From that moment on, I saw everything in a different light. And I knew what I had to do to do to get my husband back.

My first order of business was to fix things with my sons.

I sat the twins down together in the kitchen and reached across the table to grasp each of their right hands. I looked at them for a minute. My handsome boys were becoming handsome men, each resembling his father more and more each day. I loved them and had done everything in my power to give them good lives. I realized that my actions as of late had hurt them and confused their worlds as much as they had mine.

"How are you two?" I asked.

"I'm okay," Blair said softly. "How are you, Mama?"

I smiled. "Better." I turned to Morgan. "And you, Mr. Morgan. How are you?"

He dropped his eyes and shrugged. "I'm fine."

I shook my head. "No, you're not. Tell me how you feel. Tell me the truth."

He leaned back in his chair. "I'm worried about you. I'm worried about Coach. I feel like his leaving is my fault."

I tightened my grip on his hand. "No, it's not. Don't you even think that! None of this has anything to do with either of you boys. Sahib, either. It's my fault that everything is in such a mess. Do you understand why?"

Blair nodded slowly. "You and my dad?"

I sighed. This was harder than I'd ever imagined. "Yes. I was…I cheated on Coach with your dad." I couldn't think of any other way to put it.

"Are you and my dad getting back together?" Blair asked.

I leaned back in my chair. "Is that what you guys want to happen?"

Morgan cocked his head to the side. "Is that what would make you happy, Mama?"

"Honestly, I don't think so. I would always miss Coach. I want to fix things with him if he'll let me. Is that okay with you guys?"

"We just want you to be happy again, Ma," Blair offered. "We love Coach. We miss him, too. I love my dad, but I know things have always been complicated between the two of you."

He was just too smart. "Oh, so you figured that out, huh?" I said.

"Come on, Ma. We always knew Dad was married to someone else. We're not stupid," Morgan said.

"Well, Morgan, do you agree with your brother…about Coach?"

Morgan nodded. "I love him, Ma. He's my real dad, and I know he loves me. I just…I don't know why I acted so stupid with him. There's just a lot going on in my head sometimes. I know I'll never be as smart as Blair. I won't have the kind of future he will. I'm scared of disappointing you. What if I flunk out of college? You did so much to make sure we had the best. I don't want to embarrass you."

I sat up straight, released both of their hands and clasped my own together. "Oh, Morgan. Is that what all that 'see the world' talk was about? Baby, I don't expect you to be like Blair. You two might be twins, but you've never been the same person. You're two very different halves of a whole—I've always known that. If you don't want to go to college, that's your choice. I'm sorry for pressuring you. I'm sorry for a lot of the things I've done."

He gave me a hopeful look. "So, you won't be mad at me if I don't go to college?"

"Not at all. Of course I still want you to go, but if you don't, I won't be mad at you. I love you guys and I always will. No matter what happens, that will never change."

Morgan smiled. "Well, you'll be glad to know that I've decided to play ball for Coach T then."

"Really, Morgan? Are you sure?" I asked excitedly.

"Yes, ma'am. I'm gonna follow the advice my dad gave me."

"Wasif? What did he say?"

"Not him, my dad, Corey. He told me to pray about it and that if I decided to go to college he'd help me pick out a major that I could handle."

I wanted to cry, but I was working on doing less of that, so I fought the tears. "He did? When…when did you talk to him?"

"I talk to him all the time—at school or on the phone. We've actually gotten closer since he left. I apologized to him, and he told me he understood. Blair talks to him all the time, too."

I looked at Blair. "You do?"

Blair nodded in response.

I shook my head. "I miss him so much." I hadn't talked to him in weeks. He made a point of visiting Sahib at the daycare to avoid me. I wondered if he hated me just that much or if it hurt him to see me. Whichever was the case, I wanted and needed to see him. But I had some other business to take care of first.

"Do you think Sahib is coping with things okay?" I asked them.

"Yeah, I think so. He's a pretty smart kid, though. And he misses Coach, too," Blair said.

I nodded. "I know. Well, I'm going to do everything in my power to bring him back home. I promise you that."

***

Over the next few weeks, I continued my therapy and spent most of my time trying to piece my life back together. I attended church regularly—and not just to see Corey. I actually listened to the sermons. I even joined a prayer group that meets once a week and I prayed for someone other than myself. Who'd have thought that could happen?

I resumed my work at the library on a part-time basis. I cooked and cleaned and raised my sons, and I was coping, but I still missed Corey. Wasif visited Sahib often and even picked him up from daycare for me from time to time. He brought us dinner sometimes and his child support checks kept the bills paid. He didn't proposition me and he didn't threaten to take Sahib either. I think he just felt sorry for me since I'd had such a mental collapse. But the thought never left my mind that one day he could ride off to the airport with my baby and never turn around.

I knew I would have to get an actual legal custody agreement with him and I decided I needed to discuss that with him, among other things. I arrived at his doorstep on a Wednesday morning, his one and only official off day. I knocked and it took him a few minutes to open the door. When he did, I saw that his eyes were droopy and he was shirtless, wearing a pair of scrub bottoms. I'd interrupted his sleep.

"Can I talk to you for a moment?" I asked.

He nodded and backed out of the doorway. "Sure."

I sat on the sofa and watched as he sat down beside me. "Why do I have a feeling I'm not going to like what you have to say?" he asked.

I sighed. "Because you know me very well."

He rested his elbows on his knees and clasped his hands together, his eyes glued to the floor. "You and Sanders have reconciled?"

"Not yet, but I want that more than anything."

"And you came here to tell me that it's over between us?"

"Yes, and that nothing you say or threaten to do will change my mind."

He turned and looked at me. "You really love him, don't you?"

I nodded. "I really do, Wasif. More than I even realized."

"I know. I realized it when you were in the hospital. I married another woman and you didn't even blink an eye. You thought he was cheating on you and you assaulted a nurse."

I gave him a sheepish look. "Yeah, I'm sorry about that. I hope I didn't cause you any embarrassment since you work there."

He smiled. "None at all. Your last name is Sanders, not Masood, remember?"

We were both quiet for a moment, and then Wasif cleared his throat and said, "Do you hate me, Mo?"

I frowned. "No, of course I don't."

"But you don't love me, either."

I looked him in the eye. "I do love you, Wasif. I love you very much, I can't deny that."

"But you love him more."

I didn't answer him. I *couldn't* answer him.

"I see," he said with a sigh.

"Look, Wasif. I appreciate you for the role you've played in my life, in our sons' lives. You've always been good to me in your own way. But what we had is over. I belong with Corey. There's no doubt in my mind about that."

"Why?" he said softly.

"Why, what?"

"Why him? What about him makes him so special?"

"His heart."

Wasif's eyes searched the room. "I have a heart, too, Mo."

"I know. It…it just never felt like you belonged to me, Wasif. I never felt like you were totally mine. Things are different with Corey. With him, it's always been just the two of us, you know?"

"Well, you're wrong. I've never belonged to anyone but you. You've always had me—*all* of me."

Unable to find even one word to say, I remained silent.

"Anything else you need to tell me?" he asked.

I offered him a weak smile. "I hope we can truly be friends, Wasif, for the boys' sake. Especially Sahib."

He sighed as he leaned back against the sofa. "I guess I'll have to take what I can get. If the only way I can be around you is to be your friend, then I'll be your friend. But I want you to understand that I really love you, Mo. I love you with all my heart and I always will."

I closed my eyes and shook my head. "Wasif…"

He reached for my hand and clutched it tightly in his. "I mean it. I love you so much."

"Wasif, I wish things were different. I wish—"

He placed a finger to my lips to silence me. "You've already said what needs to be said. I just wanted you to know how I feel."

"I've always known, Wasif."

"Good."

I dropped my eyes. "So, are you still planning to take Sahib from me?"

Wasif leaned forward and stared at the floor. "That was never going to happen, Mo. I just…I was desperate. I needed some type of leverage. I'm sorry about that. I'd never take him from you. If nothing else, you've always been a good mother to my sons."

I frowned a little. "Oh, thank you, I guess…"

"You know what I mean. Look, I thought if we spent enough time together, things would go back to the way they used to be between us. I thought you'd realize we belonged together. I guess I was wrong."

I shook my head. "What you did was cruel, Wasif. I never thought you'd be capable of doing something like that."

"I know. I'm sorry, Mo. I really am."

After a moment of silence, I said, "I'm having a lawyer draft an official custody agreement for Sahib. I really want you to sign it. I need it if I'm going to save my marriage."

He looked at me for a moment. "Okay."

I stood to leave. "And one more thing."

With sad eyes, he said, "Yes?"

"Thank you for loving me, Dr. Wasif Masood."

He stood to face me. "Mona-Lisa Dandridge, I couldn't stop loving you if I tried," he said as he leaned in and kissed my cheek. "And if things don't work out between you and Sanders, I'll be right here waiting for you—not that I'm wishing you any ill will." He smiled.

"Wasif, you'll find someone else."

He shook his head. "I don't want to. You're the only one for me."

I smiled at him. "For what it's worth, I do kind of wish I could be with both of you."

He raised his eyebrows. "That could be arranged."

I sighed as I reached up and rubbed his cheek. "Goodbye."

He placed his hand over mine. "Goodbye, babe."

As I reached for the doorknob, he grabbed me and laid a kiss on me that left me panting and speechless.

"Uh…" I said after he released me.

He gave me lopsided grin and said, "Yeah, I'll wait."

After I regained my composure, I left his place and hesitated at the door of his neighbor—the nurse. I stood there for five or ten minutes before I knocked. She opened the door and a shocked looked spread across her face. She moved to close it, but I blocked it with my hand. She slammed the door against my hand and I yelped.

"Damn! I just wanted to apologize!" I grunted as I rubbed my throbbing hand.

The door slowly creaked open again and she stood there and stared at me.

"I'm sorry for hitting and kicking you. I was out of line and you didn't deserve that," I continued.

"You spit on me, too," she said softly.

With raised eyebrows I said, "I did? I don't remember that."

She frowned. "Well, I'm not lying. You spit on me and pulled some of my hair out of my head."

"Oh…well, I'm sorry for that, too. I really am." I turned to leave then paused and turned back to face her. "I know you and Corey didn't have anything going on, but I also know when a woman is after a man. I know you like him. I'm apologizing because I was wrong about the two of you, and it was wrong for me to attack you. But make no mistake, if you ever really go after him, I'll give you worse than I gave you the last time." I left, leaving her standing in her doorway with her mouth hanging open.

Maybe I should've left the last part off, but I just couldn't. Oh, well.

Chapter 22

"Lead Me Into Love"

When Cleo called and softly said, "I'm ready," it took a moment for my mind to register what she meant. I'd been working so hard to piece my life back together while regaining my sanity; her troubles had left my mind.

Once I realized what she was talking about, I said, "Okay. When do you want to do this?"

We hashed out the details over that phone call, and the following weekend, we met each other in Jacksonville. Cleo was the first to make it. I parked right behind her and silently prayed for the both of us. Then I climbed out of my truck and walked up to her. She grasped my hand so tightly I thought she'd break it.

We slowly walked up to the duplex and Cleo took a deep breath and tightened her death grip on my hand before knocking on the dingy door. I think we both held our breaths as we waited for an answer.

The door flung open and a short, squatty Hispanic woman stood on the other side. Were we too late? Was she already gone?

Cleo stood in frozen silence. So I spoke up. "Is...does Christina Dandridge still live here?" I asked. *Is she still alive?*

The woman nodded. "Yes, who are you?" she replied in heavily-accented English.

"We're...we're her daughters, um, Mona and Cleo," I said.

The woman's eyes lit up. "Daughters?! Yes, yes, come in! She talks about you all the time!"

I made the first step into the apartment. Cleo slowly followed.

"Come," the woman said. "I am Dulcina. Christina is my friend and I've been taking care of her. She is very sick, you know."

I nodded. "Yes."

"Well, she is in bed. Sit down and I will tell her that her beautiful daughters are here. Sit, sit."

We sat down almost in unison. I could see Cleo's eyes travelling around the dim room. Not much had changed since my last visit, other than the fact that someone had dusted the furniture and the place smelled like fresh pine cleaner instead of stale cigarette smoke.

Cleo reached for my hand again. "It looks the same," she said softly. "It's like time stood still here after I left."

I'd never thought of it that way, but that was exactly how it seemed.

Dulcina reappeared and said, "She is too weak to get up. You girls can come in here to see her."

I nodded then stood from the sofa and pulled Cleo to her feet. As I began to walk towards our mother's bedroom, I could feel Cleo's hesitation and apprehension. I felt for her, but I knew this was something she needed to do. We both needed to do it.

As we walked into the room, I almost gasped. In the three or so years since I'd last seen my mother, she'd greatly deteriorated. If she weighed a hundred pounds it would've surprised me. She was tiny and frail and almost all of her hair had turned a dirty gray color. The skin hung from her face as she looked up at us and smiled.

"Well, well, I never thought I'd see you again, Mo."

"I wanted to bring Cleo to see you," I said, not really addressing her statement.

Her eyes drifted from me to Cleo and something absolutely extraordinary happened. A tear rolled down my mother's cheek. I'd never, ever seen my mother cry. As a matter of fact, I'd never seen her show any emotion at all other than anger and hatred.

She lifted a bony hand and rested it on Cleo's cheek. "Cleo…Cleo…" she whispered.

Cleo reached up and covered Mama's hand with her own. "Yes," she whispered back. "It's me."

Mama smiled slightly. "I thought you was gone forever."

Tears flowed from Cleo's eyes as she shook her head. "No, I'm here now."

Mama reached for my hand. "Mo."

I grasped her hand. "Yes, Mama?"

"Thank you," she said, weakly.

"You're welcome," I said, and I think I actually meant it.

We stayed with Mama for an hour. We both showed her pictures of our families and Cleo even called her husband and let Mama talk to him over the phone. And when there was nothing else to say, we all just held hands. When we left, we both gave Dulcina our phone numbers. Two days later she called to tell us that our mother had passed away.

***

I walked into the gym wearing a formfitting black dress, red three-inch heels, and a bright smile. It was Corey's favorite outfit of mine and one I managed not to shred back when I lost my mind. I walked to his office door, took a deep breath, whispered a prayer, and knocked.

When he opened the door, I nearly dropped the Tupperware dish I was carrying. How could it be that this man looked even more handsome than the last time I'd seen him? It took all of the strength I could muster up not to wrap my arms around his neck and my legs around his waist. My mouth literally began to water at the sight of him. He looked *good*.

"Mona?" he said as his eyes took me in, inch by inch. Yeah, he'd missed me, too.

I held the dish out towards him. "I made some chicken enchiladas for dinner, and I remembered how much you like them, so I brought you some for lunch. There's enough for your dinner, too."

He took the dish from me, stared at me for a few seconds, and then he said, "Thank you."

"You're welcome."

I turned and slowly walked away from the office. I could feel his eyes on me as I put a little extra twist in my step. I smiled for the entire drive home.

I took him lunch every day for the next two weeks. I always smiled and he always thanked me. I didn't ask him to come home. I didn't say much of anything, actually. I just cooked all of his favorite food, wore his favorite clothes and adorned myself with his favorite perfume. After two weeks, he actually smiled and one day he said, "See you tomorrow." That was enough to make my heart leap.

I also started sending him text messages every morning. In the messages I'd tell him I loved him and list one thing I missed about him. One message read:

I love you and I miss hearing you sing off-key in the shower every morning.

-Mona

The third week, in addition to taking him lunch and sending the messages, I started inviting him to dinner at the house, and on that Friday, he finally accepted. He ate with us Friday, Saturday, and Sunday. After dinner, we watched TV as a family. We all laughed and talked, and it felt like our family had never been apart. The next week, I started staying and eating lunch with him in his office upon his invitation, and we actually talked. We talked about the boys and his physical training business, and my sister, and my mother, and Coach T—anything and everything but our marriage. I was just happy to be in his presence and to see him smile and to hear his voice. I was confident the rest would come in time.

And it did. One afternoon, when we were having lunch in his office, he asked, "So what are we doing, Mona?"

I looked up at him and smiled. "We're eating lunch, I think."

He shook his head. "No, me and you—what are we *doing*?"

I tilted my head to the side. "I hope we're reconciling."

He was quiet for a long while, and then he said, "Mona, I…"

I leaned forward in my chair. "Corey, before you tell me why that can't happen, can I just say something?"

He nodded, keeping his eyes on his desk.

"Look, I know I'm not perfect. I've always had issues, you know that. I'm selfish and I try to be controlling, but you won't let me."

He looked up at me and smiled.

"But the one thing you should know is that you mean the world to me. I made a mistake, Corey. *A huge mistake.* And that mistake was taking you for granted. I knew you loved me and I counted on you forgiving me for anything I did. I'm sorry. I will never take you for granted ever again."

I waited for him to respond, but he didn't. He just sat there and stared at me.

"Corey, do you still love me?" I asked.

He sighed. "More than I can say."

I felt such relief that I could've jumped up and run a marathon.

"And I wish that was enough, but it's never been enough," he added, deflating me in an instant.

"Corey, I love you and I know the words are not enough, but I plan to show you how much I love you if you'll give me a chance. I even have a legal custody agreement for Sahib. Wasif can only see him at scheduled times now. No more popping up whenever he wants to. No more disrespecting you or your home."

"A custody agreement? Really?"

"Yes. If you just give me a chance, I will show you how serious I am about making things work between us," I said eagerly.

"Can I finish what I was saying before?" he asked.

I sunk back in my chair. "I'm sorry. Go ahead."

"From the time you left the good doctor, I've never been sure if you really loved me. Even when we got married, I still questioned it. It took a long time for me to believe that you loved me and not him. So when you had the….the affair, it was like my worst fear came true. And it hurt, Mona."

"I know. *I'm so sorry.* You might not believe this, but I think I hurt myself more than I hurt you."

"I don't see how that's possible. I only *thought* you hurt me back in college. But this time…you almost destroyed me. I don't know if I'll ever get over this."

I sat back in my chair as I realized I was losing this battle. We weren't going to reconcile. He was still too hurt. It was over. *It was over.*

We sat in silence for so long that I wondered if either of us would ever speak again. Finally, I stood from the chair and swung my purse over my shoulder. "Well, I guess I'll be going," I said, my voice breaking with every word. "I won't bother you anymore, Corey. I just…I love you. I really do."

I slowly moved to the door, opened it, and walked out. I furiously blinked back tears as I quickened my pace. I made it through the building in record time and as I strode across the parking lot to my car, I let my tears fall. I gulped air and sniffled as I unlocked my door and as I opened it, I heard someone calling my name. "Mona! Wait!"

I turned to see Corey running in my direction.

I just stood there, hoping against hope that this was it. Was he coming home?

He finally caught up with me and as he caught his breath, I wiped my face and tried to pull myself together.

"I've been praying," he said breathily. "I've been praying for God to take you out of my heart. I've prayed and prayed to stop loving you. But I can't. I think about you all the time. I miss you like hell, Mona."

I closed my eyes. "I know how you feel."

"I…I've been to my lawyer's office so many times I lost count. He drew up the divorce papers weeks ago, but I just haven't been able to bring myself to have them filed."

I just stood there in stunned silence.

"Mona, I need to know something."

"*Anything.*"

"What would you do if I told you we could never be together again?"

I leaned against the car, suddenly feeling my legs weaken. "Um, I'd be hurt—no—*devastated.* I guess I'd eventually go on with my life, but I'd always love you. I would always miss you. Now, that's what my therapist would want me to say."

"Therapist?"

I nodded. "It's a long story. Do you want to know what I'd *really* do?

"Yes," he softly said.

"I would do what I've been doing since you left. I would feel like I lost the best thing that ever happened to me. I would pray nonstop for you to forgive me. I would spend most of my nights awake in bed, going out of my mind missing you and wanting to die at the thought of you being with someone else. I'd sit and stare at your picture on the dresser. I'd close my eyes and think about you. I'd wrack my brain trying to relive every moment I ever spent with you. I would touch my lips, trying to feel your kisses. I would buy a bottle of your favorite cologne and spray it in the room, just so I could smell you. I would hug myself and pretend that my arms are yours. But I would never, *ever* stop loving you."

I saw the tears in his eyes as he said, "You do those things?"

"All the time."

Corey searched my eyes. "You love me that much?" he asked.

"Baby, I'm not perfect by far, but you could search the world over and you'd never find a woman who loves you more than I do."

"And you're serious about the custody thing?"

"Yes. I have the papers in the car if you want to see them."

He pulled his cell phone from his pocket and began dialing a number or texting or something. What the hell?

"Um, Corey, what—"

He held up his hand. "Give me a minute," he said, never taking his eyes off of the phone.

So I just stood there like an idiot, my temper rising by the second. Who or what was so important that he had to pull out his phone in the middle of *this* conversation?

He finished whatever he was doing, shoved the phone back in his pocket, and looked up at me. "Check your phone," he said.

My hand trembled as I dug the phone out of my purse. There was one new message—from Corey. I clicked the button and the message appeared on the screen:

I love you and I miss everything about you. I'm ready.

-Corey

I looked up at him through a haze of tears. "Does this mean you—we…"

He moved closer to me. "It means I realize I played a role in our marriage falling apart. I should've spent more time at home—with you. With our family. And I'm sorry about what I said about the boys. I love them and I *am* their father."

"It's okay."

"And…and I'm willing to try again."

"You are?"

He nodded. "Yes. You think your therapist would be willing to counsel us as a couple?"

I wiped my wet cheeks. "Yes, she would. Thank you. Thank you so much. You won't regret this. I promise."

"Look, I'm not promising you anything. I'm willing to try again, but we have to take this slow, Mona."

"We can crawl if you want to."

Chapter 23

"Feel The Need"

I don't think a mother ever felt as proud as I did the day Corey, Wasif, and I stood behind Morgan and Blair and watched them sign their letters of intent. Well, Wasif actually stood to the side of us, keeping his distance from Corey. Coach T looked rather pleased as well. Sahib sat on Corey's shoulders with a big grin on his face. Everything was going well. It took weeks of therapy and hours upon hours of prayer—I'm talking about flat-on-my-face prayer—but my husband was finally back home, and I was so happy.

After the newspapers took their pictures, I scurried off to the restroom and then made a pit stop at a water fountain. I was startled by a voice behind me.

"Mrs. Sanders, I was hoping I'd get to speak with you today." It was Coach T.

Lord, I hope he is not planning to hit on me or something. I pasted on a smile and said, "Oh, really? How can I help you?"

He cleared his throat and rocked back on his heels. "I just wanted you to know that I am thrilled to have your boys on my team. They are some great young men. You should be proud."

"Well, I am. I'm *very* proud of them."

I moved to walk past him and he said, "And you should be proud of yourself, too. You are a beautiful, intelligent woman."

Oh, dear Lord. He really is trying to hit on me. I frowned slightly. "Um, thanks. I'd, uh, better get back to my *husband*, now."

I began to walk away and he grasped my arm to stop me. My frown deepened as I said, "Look, I don't know what your deal is, but you've seen my husband. I don't think you wanna get on his bad side."

He kept his hand on my arm and said, "Um, my name's Michael…Michael Tolliver."

I rolled my eyes. "Yeah, well, nice to meet you. I'm Mrs. Sanders and I gotta go because *Mr.* Sanders is waiting for me. You remember him? Tall, handsome, lots of muscles?"

"Mona-Lisa, I'm your father."

His hand dropped and so did my jaw.

Michael Tolliver…Michael Tolliver… That was my father's name, but the last time I'd seen him, he was young…and naked. I looked at the man in front of me and tried to see myself in his face. I stared at him for a long while. In fact, we stared at each other. We stood there for so long that Corey came looking for me. When he found me, he slipped an arm around my waist and kissed my cheek. "I've been looking all over for you," he said.

I turned and looked at Corey, then back at Coach T—Michael Tolliver—my father. It was him. I was sure of it. I had his ears and his mouth. He was my father. The man who'd left me to be raised by a horrible, hateful woman and only showed up once in my entire childhood and that was just so he could sleep with my mother—the man who stood in a bathroom naked as a jaybird and peed while me and my little sister watched. He never sent me a Christmas gift or a birthday card. Hell, he never even called to say hi in all of my thirty-six years of living. And here he stood, looking healthy and happy— calling himself my father.

I balled up my fists. I wanted to punch him in the mouth and then I wanted to knee him in the groin. And after that, I wanted to call him everything but a child of God. *I hated him.*

Corey looked down at my fists and then up at Coach T. "Mona, what's going on?"

I stepped right into my father's personal space and said, "Corey, I want you to meet my father or at least that's who he says he is, although he'd have to strip naked and start peeing in order for me to be sure."

Coach T dropped his eyes in embarrassment.

"What?!" Corey said, pulling me back a little. "You're her father?"

Coach T nodded. "Yes, I've been wanting to meet her for a while."

"Well, damn, I'm not hard to find. I've lived in the same state my whole life! And I surely wasn't hard to find when I was a child. You didn't have any problem navigating your way to my mama's sofa or between her legs, did you? And you made it into that bathroom and showed me all of your business with no difficulty at all!" My words oozed out like venom. Yes, I *hated* this man.

"I'm very sorry about that. I was…I was young and stupid. I wouldn't have been a good father to you back then."

"So what you gonna do? Father me now? I'm a grown-ass woman!"

"I was hoping you'd help me with something."

"Help you? *Help you?* Are you for damn real? What the hell could you possibly think I'd help your dead-beat behind with?!"

Corey continued to pull on my arm, inching me backwards. "Mona, calm down. Baby, please calm down," he said softly.

I took a deep breath and tried to calm myself. "Corey, get me the hell out of here before I claw this man's eyeballs out."

Corey did just that, and as he steered me down the hall, Coach T called after us. "I'm dying!"

We both stopped in our tracks. I turned around and said, "Aren't we all?"

"But I mean, I don't have long now."

"You look perfectly healthy to me," I said.

"I need a kidney. If I don't get one, I'll have to start dialysis."

"Then you're not dying."

"*Please*, help me."

I began to walk back towards him with Corey right on my heels. "My mother was horrible to me. Sometimes I never even knew where my next meal was coming from. She let one of her friends molest me while she smoked and drank with her friends in the next room. When *I* needed *you*, where were you?"

"I'm sorry, Mona-Lisa. I didn't know any of that happened to you."

"And my one and only memory of you is just as disgusting as anything she ever did to me."

"I'm…I'm sorry."

"You come sniffing around my sons acting like you want them to play ball for you and all the while, you wanted me to let some doctor saw me open and take out my freakin' kidney? And for what? *For you?!* You have never given me the time of day and you think I'm gonna give you my damn kidney?!" I smiled. "Now I know where I get my craziness from, because you must be out of your damn mind!" I grabbed Corey's hand. "Let's go."

As we walked away, I felt not a single stitch of remorse. Maybe I should've helped him. I guess that would've been the right thing to do. But I never said I was perfect.

For more information on Christian Counselors, visit:

http://www.aacc.net/resources/find-a-counselor/

For more information about the author, visit:

http://adriennethompsonwrites.webs.com

Check out the Been So Long website:

http://beensolongbooks.webs.com

You can contact Adrienne at: tapestrywriter@gmail.com

Like **Author Adrienne Thompson** on Facebook

Follow Adrienne on Twitter: https://twitter.com/A_H_Thompson

Follow Adrienne on Pinterest: http://pinterest.com/ahthompsn/

Excerpt from *Your Love is King*

Coming soon…

"You enjoying your drink?" he asked. I was taken aback by the fact that he sounded like a black man when he spoke.

"Um, yes, I am," I answered.

He smiled, revealing two rows of perfectly white teeth. His blue eyes sparkled as he spoke. "Good, I thought you might want another one."

I nearly choked. "You mean, *you* bought this drink for me?"

He nodded. "Yeah and I'd like to buy you dinner one day, too."

I looked around at my table mates and smiled. Were they pulling a fast one on me?

"Oh no, is this a joke?" I asked.

His brow furrowed. "No, why?"

"Well, I haven't ever been approached by a guy like you before," I replied, choosing my words carefully.

"What? A trumpet player? Don't tell me you've got something against dating musicians," he asked, with a serious look on his face.

Damn, I'm gonna have to come on out and say it, I thought. "No, I mean a…a white guy. I've only ever dated black men, you know?"

He leaned closer to me and said, "Oh, so you have something against dating white men?"

I leaned back and frowned. "Well no, that's not what I'm saying. I mean, I've just never dated outside of my race before. That's all."

He gave me a lopsided grin and said, "Maybe it's time for you to try some new things. Uh, what's your name, by the way? Mine's Chris. Chris King."

I returned his smile without even realizing it. "Um, it's Marli."

"Marley. Like Bob Marley?"

I nodded. "Yeah, but it's actually short for Marlena."

"Oh, that's cool, like the actress."

"Yeah, but spelled differently."

"I like it. So about that dinner…" Boy, was he persistent. He seemed nice enough and he was cute but I just couldn't see myself dating him.

"Look, Chris. Thanks for the drink, but—"

He held up his hand, "But you don't date white men. Okay, okay. I get it. Well, enjoy the rest of your drink and the rest of your evening, Ms. Marli," he said. Then as he stood to leave, he leaned over and whispered, "You have no idea what you're missing."

Excerpt from *Blues In The Key Of B (Bluesday Book III)*

Coming soon...

Faith's shrill cries awakened me from a shallow sleep. I quickly stumbled to my feet and shuffled across the room to her crib. She had her own room, but it was just easier to let her sleep in our bedroom. After three months of midnight diaper changes and feedings, I should've been used to this, but I wasn't. As a singer, I'd lost count of how many all-nighters I'd pulled with concerts and after-parties, and after-after-parties. But this was different. There was no music and this was not fun for me. I was so tired and my wonderful, handsome, loving husband was proving to be little to no help.

I gently lifted my little girl into my arms, sat in the rocking chair next to her crib, and began to breast-feed her. I looked down at her and sighed. She was a beautiful little combination of me and Reggie with soft brown skin and curly black hair. I leaned my head back against the chair and closed my eyes. I hated feeling this way, resenting having to care for my own child—a child Reggie and I fervently prayed for. But despite my best efforts to shake my feelings, I couldn't.

I opened my eyes and looked over at Reggie who hadn't so much as moved a muscle. It was unfair. It really was. I had no choice but to get up every time the baby woke up. I was breast-feeding her. I *had* to get up. And though breast-feeding had been a mutual decision, I couldn't help but feel like I'd gotten the short end of the stick.

Tears began to fill my eyes. *What is wrong with me? Why do I feel this way?* I wondered as I blinked back tears and took a deep breath. Three months had passed and I still felt the same way I'd felt when we first brought Faith home—detached. I felt like I was holding someone else's baby. I didn't feel like her mother. I didn't feel like *anyone's* mother for that matter. There was no connection. No bond. Sure, I fed her and changed her and bathed her, but those things felt more like chores than motherhood. When was my motherly instinct going to kick in? When was I going to start to love my baby?

I gently pulled her from my breast, and held her against my chest to burp her. I breathed in her fresh scent and looked down at her little body and wished I knew what was wrong with me. *Maybe I'm crazy. Maybe I need to see a shrink.* I quickly dismissed those thoughts. How could I explain to Reggie and then a doctor that I didn't love my own child? They'd surely have me committed. No, this was something I'd just have to figure out how to deal with on my own. I'd just have to make myself love her.

She burped softly and then rested her little head against my shoulder. I closed my eyes and rocked a few more minutes before placing her back into her crib then returning to bed. As I settled in under the covers, Reggie draped his arm across my waist and snuggled close to me.

"Everything okay?" he asked.

I stared across the room through the darkness at the crib. "Everything's fine," I lied.

www.ingramcontent.com/pod-product-compliance
Lightning Source LLC
Chambersburg PA
CBHW070017260626
47159CB00005B/1844